Lily

Without

By Guillermo Paxton

Copyright © 2021 WCP Publishing Company

Printed in the United States of America

Lily Without/ Paxton — 2nd Edition

ISBN: 9780977199389

1.Title 2. Drama. 3. Juárez, México. 4. Erotica . 5. Thriller 6. Prostitution. 7. Corruption. 8. WCP Publishing - Fiction

Dedicated to the victims of violence in all of Mexico, especially to the women of Juarez.

*Had it lived long, it would have been
Lilies without, roses within.*

— From *The Nymph Complaining for the
Death of her Fawn* by Andrew Marvell

1

Lila peered at her reflection in the bathroom mirror, as she found herself doing more and more as she aged. The crow's feet in the eyes looked ever more pronounced, her lines of expression ever deeper, and every time she looked into the mirror, she was always able to find a new wrinkle or flaw in her aspect. She sighed as she touched up the blue-grey mascara on her eyelids. Outside of the bathroom "Stairway to Heaven" was playing on the jukebox in the bar where she had spent the last five years working. The light in the bathroom was brighter than that of the bar and less for- giving, allowing Lila to see her true image, not the dimmed-down reddish tone version that the clients saw. The poor light quality being a blessing for the women who worked in bars like these, blurring the blemishes, stretch marks, and cellulite. She entered the stall, lifted her skirt, pulled down her thong in one fluid motion, and sat on the toilet and peed. She dried herself, patting from front to back, and lifted her thong back into place. She rinsed her hands, straightened her skirt, and after one last look in the mirror, exited the bathroom with her best game face.

"Oh baby, you look great!" The older gringo wearing a worn-out t-shirt with a cartoon of a fisherman catching bass said to her as she sat back down at the table. He spoke out of the right side of his mouth, a cigar tightly held in his lips on the left side, smoky trails following his words. An imprint of a boat was warped by the stretching of the t-shirt over his beer belly. His friend was younger and in better physical shape, and was buying drinks for a younger woman that Lila worked with, Valeria. Lila had given Valeria a lot of advice over the last year, the best being not to ever fall for a client. Lila had seen many a younger woman take a client on as a boyfriend and end up burned later, after they found out that he was married or had some other commitment. Lila had taught Valeria many tricks of the trade, including how to make more money with the drinks without seeming greedy.

"You just tell the waiter to bug you every few minutes, as if he's insisting you drink more. Then you apologize to the client and let them know that you really like them, but that your boss is a real bastard. Don't have any mercy with them, Valeria. Your good looks and youth won't last forever, so get the most out of them while you can," she had told Valeria the first week she had gotten to the Pink Lady.

Gringos were a rare commodity in Juarez since the drug war had hit with intensity in 2008, so Lila and Valeria were the envy of all the other girls at the Pink Lady bar. Only a few of the older clients, like Boat-belly, were die-hard clients and still visited Juarez on occasion, their vices overwhelming their fears of the violent city that Juarez had become. Valeria had the other man enamored and he was buying her two drinks for every one drink that Lila was bought. She couldn't drink as fast or she would make the old gringo Boat-belly angry and he'd dump her for a younger one. She had to really pour on the charm, too. He smelled like cigar and his mouth was a stagnant pool of smoke, peanuts and whiskey. It made her want to vomit, but she managed through the nausea and got yet another drink. The waiter brought her the ficha, a yellow paper with her name on it that she would later trade in for her commission, a dollar for every drink bought for her. Boat-belly said something in English to her and laughed, and so she laughed too, even though she had no idea what he had said.

"Cuanto es?" He asked her, referring to how much it would be for sex.

"Forty-five dollars. Fifty-five for oral, sixty-five for anal." Boat-belly opened his wallet and counted out sixty-five dollars. He wanted to hand it to Lila, but she mimed that he would have to give it to the waiter so they could go to the rooms upstairs from the bar. He understood and she called the waiter over. Boat-belly and the waiter hashed out the details, and the man gave the waiter an extra ten dollars so that he wouldn't be bothered after about fifteen minutes, the point at which the waiter would usually knock on the door and say "tiempo" which meant that the client would have to finish in a hurry. Lila led Boat-belly to the room that she normally used, and closed the door behind them both.

With older, out of shape men, the challenge would usually be to just get a rise out of them, literally. Lila had worked her fifteen minutes many a time only to get a client semi-hard and ending up doing nothing with them. The reality was that most of the time the clients were too drunk, stoned, and/or old to get it up, which was fine by her. They just wanted to look good in front of their buddies. Boat-belly turned out to be no exception, and after about twenty minutes he gave up. She told him not to worry, and when they got back to his table, she made a sign to Valeria that he was a well-endowed man and Boat-belly smiled. Her friend looked at him and mouthed the word "wow", and his buddy nodded approvingly and gave his older friend the thumbs up. Boat-belly was impressed and relieved, and he bought Lila another few drinks while his buddy was busy with Valeria. It was closing time when Valeria and Boat-belly's buddy came back downstairs. The clients said goodbye, and Lila kissed Boat-belly on the cheek and Valeria followed her lead. Lila and Valeria cashed in their fichas for their share of the drinks' profit, and they exited to the parking lot through the back door and got into Lila's Explorer that was parked in a secure area guarded by an older man that had probably worked there for centuries. Valeria gave Lila five dollars for gas, and Lila dropped her off at her apartment and drove home. Her two children were asleep on the couch by her neighbor, an older woman who used to be a prostitute but now worked as a cashier at a corner grocery store, was watching a soap opera.

"How did it go?" Lila handed her the five dollars that Valeria had given to her.

"Not bad. Thanks for looking after them."

"Anytime," her neighbor smiled, taking the money. She left, and after putting the girls to bed, Lila took a long, hot shower, imagining that the water had the power to wash away both the stink of men and her unwanted wrinkles away, leaving her clean and youthful again. She looked in the mirror as she dried off and the wrinkles remained, but the stink was gone, even if only temporarily. She went back into the girls' bedroom and watched them sleep. Yamileth was nine years old and Carmen was seven. Lila had divorced their father shortly after Carmen's birth. He was abusive and a drunkard. She never received a dime of child support, and a lawyer was too cost prohibitive for her to really do anything about it. They were good girls and they had no idea that their mother worked as a prostitute. She caressed their faces gently with her fingertips and remembered when she was a young girl without a worry about money or a thought about sex and she sighed. In the morning she would have to go to her second job- the massage parlor.

2

Lila was on top of the man that had just paid her to have sex with him, the massage table they were on rocking with her up and down movement. She made some noise so that the man would think she was enjoying his semi-hard member inside of her. Had she not been an expert, she would never have been able to put the condom on his flaccid member. The man suddenly orgasmed; his body rigid and his teeth clenched, he moaned and groaned, and he was finished. Lila grabbed the condom at the base of the member and dismounted so that the condom did not slide off into her and hopped off the table. She took some toilet paper from the roll and handed it to him. He cleaned himself off.

"I'll prepare your shower. Hot, warm or cool?" "Hot."

Lila turned the knobs and stuck her hand into the water, adjusting until it became comfortably hot. She motioned that the shower was ready and the man jumped in. While he showered, she took the sheet off the massage table and wiped the table down with disinfectant. When he got out, she jumped in and quickly washed her breasts and pussy and anywhere else that the man had touched or put his mouth upon. She turned the water off and dried off with a towel she kept at the massage parlor especially for her. She slipped on a summer dress and the man finished dressing and scrambled around in his wallet deciding how much he would tip her. He pulled out ten dollars and Lila took it, remembering when her tips were twenty and above, but hardly ungrateful since many men didn't even tip at all. When he left, she pulled out a cigarette and lit it. The other two women in the massage parlor were busy so she had the small lobby with five chairs to herself. Lila stood and looked outside of the one-way mirror windows at the people driving to the drive-up window of the Church's Chicken that was next to the massage parlor. She was hungry, but fried chicken was the last thing that she would eat, grease being her mortal enemy. The other two women eventually finished with their clients and joined her in the lobby, talking to each other while ignoring her. She was in charge while the boss was away, having been there the longest, and the other women at the Roma massage parlor resented her for that. They hated her when she was in charge, when she had a good client, when a new man picked her over them, which happened less and less frequently. Even though she was by far the most experienced in the parlor, most men preferred youth, and that, coupled with the terrible economy and lack of security in Juarez, had led to Lila getting the second job at the Pink Lady at nights. She ignored the two girls' glares and finished her cigarette. A well-dressed, muscular man knocked on the door of the Roma. "Oh my God, my prayers have been answered!" said one of the other women. Lila unlocked the glass door and let the man in. He smiled at her and she smiled back. "Hi. Would you like information?" "Yes".

"One hour, forty dollars, includes massage and vaginal relations with the girl. Oral and anal you have to negotiate with the girl." The man smiled again, sat down and took in the three women with his big brown eyes. He kept looking at the youngest woman and Lila sat down, feeling defeated by her age. The man asked the younger woman if she knew how to massage well. She said she would make him happy, but he insisted that she answer who in the Roma knew how to do a really good actual massage. Both the women pointed at Lila, because she really did know how. "Okay then, let's go," he said, looking at Lila. She saw the other two women leering at her through her peripheral vision and she smiled slightly, happily accepting the small victory. She even took the client by his hand while she led him to the massage room just to make her coworkers even more jealous. The man followed behind her, oblivious of the envy and jealousy that he was the cause of.

Lila closed the door of the small room behind her and turned to the man. He was already getting undressed, not shy at all, taking off his shirt, pants, and underwear in just a few fluid motions. Lila appreciated the work he obviously put into his body, but she was not particularly attracted to him. She had not been attracted to men for years, sometime between just after her divorce and when she started working at the Roma. Her first experience with a woman had been with the woman in charge of the Roma at that time. The sex had blown her mind. "You can lay face down on the table." She told the man who promptly followed her instruction. His naked body was flawless and it made her smile because she knew that either of the other two women would have had sex with this man for free. She gave him the best massage she could, using plenty of oil, starting at the neck and shoulders and slowly working her way down. She had him turn over and he was very erect. She continued the massage from the chest and shoulders to his arms, and then to his abdomen and down the legs to his feet. She asked if he wanted to have sexual relations, and he said that a hand job was fine. She was relieved that he had suggested the hand job. The man was hung and Lila had not handled anything like that in years, maybe ever. She cleaned him up, unlike the other man, mainly because this man was much cleaner and hand jobs were so much better for her than having to have sex, regardless of the penis size. He turned and looked at her.

"I have a question."

She didn't answer right away and the man stayed quiet, just looking at her. "Okay. Ask."

"I have a beautiful wife. We have been involved with some trios, a few young ladies, and she enjoys being with other women, but so far, she hasn't been with the right one. I am looking for a lesbian, a real lesbian, one that can really make her happy. If you understand what I am saying." He paused, his stare penetrating into Lila's core being. She shuddered, and he continued. "Do you know anyone that would be good for this? I'd like to hire her and watch. Not join, just watch."

Lila's heart raced for a moment. She didn't know why; she had been with women and in trios many times before. "Actually, I do. I prefer women."

The man smiled. "Really? That's perfect. Do you have a lot of experience, can you make her really, really happy?" He spoke quickly, feverishly, and he was obviously aroused again.

"Oh, I am sure I can. I handled you well, right? If I can handle you, think how much better I can handle a woman, knowing a woman's body as intimately as I do. I have plenty of experience. I know how to make a woman very happy."

The man was rock hard and he smiled. They discussed for a while how they could get together, and finally agreed that he would bring his wife to the Roma for a "massage" and that he would stay in the lobby while she massaged his wife. Lila was excited and hoped that the man was not a flake like so many customers were.

He had shown her a photograph of his wife and she truly was beautiful. And sexy.

3

Lila had almost forgotten the well-built man and his beautiful wife, and was pleasantly surprised to see them appear at the glass door three weeks later. Lila's heart skipped a beat as she let the couple in and saw how really gorgeous the woman was. If the woman had presented herself as a Victoria's Secret model, no one would ever have questioned it. She was wearing jean shorts that barely covered her round buttocks, and a sleeveless top that was tight to her perfect abdomen. Her legs were thick and muscular like those of a dancer, and her arms were toned. Her hair was naturally black and long, and it flowed over her shoulders and back. Her breasts were round and full and Lila noticed that her nipples were already erect. Lila closed and locked the front door after they entered, turned and stared at the woman. When Lila looked up at her face again, she realized that she had been staring for a lot longer than she had realized and, blushing, she looked down at her own feet to contemplate the meaning of her leather sandals. The well-built man smiled, pleased that Lila was smitten with his wife.

"She's all yours." Lila blushed and took the woman by her hand and led her to the massage cubicle. She shut the door and locked it, and turned to take in the beauty of this lady that had been brought to her. She smiled and shook out her hand and the beautiful woman took it.

"My name's Lila. It is very nice to meet you."

"I'm Julia. Likewise." Her green eyes sparkled.

"You can put your clothes here," she said, pointing to a chair near the massage table, "and just lay face down. I'll take care of the rest." Julia appeared to be nervous.

"Don't worry. You're not the first woman to come to me for a massage. I have several women who come on a regular basis. I think it's because I'm doing a decent job. I promise I'll do my best for you."

Julia undressed in front of Lila, carefully folding up each garment and placing it carefully onto the chair. Her nipples were hard. Lila felt herself become moist. Julia positioned herself onto the massage table, face down. Lila ran her fingers from Julia's right foot slowly up her leg and over her butt, gently across her back to her neck. Goosebumps, for both women. She picked up a bottle of oil and dropped a bit into her hands and began at Julia's shoulders, her white hands even lighter against Julia's darker hue. Julia moaned gently, quietly. Lila continued on, without hurry, over her deltoids and back to the shoulders and neck. She climbed onto the table and mounted Julia, just where her legs met her buttocks. Then she rubbed from the top of her buttocks all the way to her shoulders and back again with long, slow strokes. Julia sighed, a pleasureful sound that informed Lila that she approved of the massage thus far.

Lila turned around on the table, placing her buttocks onto Julia's lower back. She worked Julia's buttocks and thighs, and down her legs. She rubbed as close to her vaginal lips as she could without actually touching them. Lila could have spent all day on Julia's butt; it was the most perfect one she had ever seen, much less touch.

She dismounted and worked on Julia's well- kept, long, and slender feet. Her toenails were just the right length and were painted pink, matching her fingernails. Julia was enjoying the foot massage immensely and Lila made a mental note that she had sensitive feet. She asked Julia to turn over and she complied. Lila took in the sight. Julia's breasts were round and firm, like her butt. Her nipples were still hard. Her abdomen was perfectly sculpted, not too much like a bodybuilder, but the outlines of the six-pack were noticeable. Her entire body was completely hairless. Even her pussy was pretty, the lips symmetrical and well-formed, her large, swollen clitoris perfect. Lila turned and mounted again, just below the waist, and began massaging her arms, her hands shoulders and then her breasts. Julia's rock- like nipples felt delicious as she ran them between her fingers. She continued the massage to her abdomen, and lower still, to her inner thighs. She saw that a crystalline liquid was forming in between Julia's labia. She leaned over and began to kiss Julia's neck, her breasts, teasing the already firm nipples with her tongue and her lips. While she worked her breasts, she reached down and gently played with her well-lubricated clitoris. She worked it between her thumb and forefinger as she sucked on Julia's breasts and nipples. Julia came, a small orgasm that made her entire body shudder for an instant. Lila moved down to lick her, but the massage table was too small, so she dismounted.

"Darling, this table is way too small. Let me put a sheet on the floor and we can have more room.

Julia nodded and hopped off the table. Lila was pissed that she had to break the moment, but there was no way she would have been able to double over to do what she wanted. Julia lay down onto the floor and Lila got back to where she was, but from the side. She worked down from her breasts to her clitoris with her lips and tongue. It was not normally what she would have done, but this woman was so clean, so perfect, Lila couldn't help herself. She worked her clitoris with her tongue, suctioning with her lips, and slid her finger into Julia's wet pussy. She turned her finger upwards and hit her G-spot. She made her orgasm within just a few minutes, and she continued through to another. She would have gone for a third but one of the other women knocked on the door because Lila had gone way past the hour allotted.

"I'm sorry, mi Reyna. Time is up. I would have liked to have had more."

Julia smiled. "It's fine. I'm quite satisfied."

Lila loved the way her green eyes glowed and the way her lips pursed as she said purred the word "satisfied". She saddened at the thought that she might never see Julia again. She prepared the shower for her and while Julia bathed, she wrote on a piece of paper her name and number. When Julia was dry and dressed, she handed the paper to her.

"I hope I will see you again." Julia smiled again. "Count on it."

4

Felix Cañez sat at his desk in the judiciales, the judicial building where arrestees were brought for questioning and then temporarily held in large holding cells, where people could make statements and depositions against others who had committed a crime, and report missing persons. He looked at the pictures on the desk of he and his wife, Julia, after he had graduated from the Juarez police academy; another picture showed when he had been promoted to judicial, a detective at state level. His partner, Rafael Martinez, or Rafa, opened the office door. He had tamales in his hand.

He always had food in his hands.

"Damn Rafa, do you ever stop eating?"

Rafa's mouth was full and he opened it to talk. "Want some?" He mumbled, and crumbs of masa, cornmeal, flew out.

"Yuck, Rafa! When civilians call us pigs, I get offended, but you truly resemble one."

Rafa laughed, more masa flying out. "Hey, you have your vices, I have mine, Güero."

Everyone called Felix "Güero". He was light skinned with blue eyes, the only one in his family, and they called him Güerito or Güero for as long as he could recollect. The women always told him how much they loved his eyes. His dad had always treated him differently from his brothers, cold and distant, unlike his warm demeanor with the rest of the family. Even though they had never spoken about it, Felix was sure that his father suspected that Felix's mother had been unfaithful with one of the travelling Mormons that often had stopped by the house for lunch. His mother, a dark-skinned woman with Indian features, had taken to feeding whatever young Mormons that showed up on their doorstep, and she was always very friendly, a bit too friendly, with the handsome ones. Whether something had happened or not, Felix's father died of Cirrhosis when he was a teenager, and the whole business was buried with him.

Rafa turned and closed the door. He wiped his mouth with a dirty handkerchief he kept in his pocket, and got close to Felix to whisper to him. "Güero, El Indio wants to meet with us later."

"What time?"

"At five. Same place as last time."

Felix never liked meeting with El Indio, the man in charge of the Juarez Plaza, the local leader of the Juarez cartel, but it would mean a pocketful of cash and, with a wife and two girlfriends to support, he needed all the cash he could get his hands on. He nodded, agreeing to the meet, knowing full well that he had no say in the matter either way. The phone on his desk rang, and both men jumped slightly, then laughed at each other.

"Cañez speaking." The voice on the other end was that of his captain. Felix nodded and said yes several times, then ended with, "Understood." He got up and checked his weapon. "What's the 10-11 with the 12?" Rafa asked using code.

"A 6-4 in process." Felix told Rafa, meaning an unknown crime was in progress.

The partners quickly made their way to a grey Dodge Ram and Felix drove them to a particularly bad area, La Chaveña, close to a place that they often stopped for flautas, La Pila. A thin young man with a backpack and dressed in baggy pants and a dirty T-shirt was walking hastily, and did his best to pretend that he did not see the judiciales driving slowly up to him. When they got closer, he began to sprint down an alley. Felix was by far in better shape than Rafa, and, placing the Ram into park, he jumped out of the vehicle and ran after the man, his nine-millimeter pistol in hand. Rafa slid into the driver's side and drove around the corner as fast as he could to reach the other end of the alley. The young man had almost made it to the end, but stopped promptly when he saw Rafa pull out his assault rifle and aim the barrel at him. The man lifted his hands and Felix tackled him at the knees. He then proceeded to punch the suspect in the back of the head, who ineffectively tried to block the blows with his hands, a nearly impossible task since he was face down.

"Why were you running, fucker! You don't ever run from me!"

Rafa was laughing as Felix punished the man, repeatedly punching and kicking him. Rafa yelled out to Felix. "Hey, that's good man. That's enough, you'll kill the bastard."

Felix had a smile on his face, a terrible grin of pleasure, and it disappeared when he realized that Rafa was correct. He pulled off the man's backpack and threw it to Rafa who immediately proceeded to search through it. He pulled out a brick of marijuana, and held it up so Felix could see. Felix nodded, handcuffed the man and finished searching him. He picked him up by the crook in his arm and punched him in the kidney- just for good measure. The man doubled over but Felix held onto his arm tightly and moved him towards the truck.

They would now proceed to the outskirts of town where they could "talk" to the man and see who he worked for. If he worked for anyone besides La Linea, which was highly probable, they would kill him and dump his body somewhere for all to see, as they had done with many others.

5

Julia knew she had to eat some protein or she would start losing muscle, but the thought of food made her nauseous. She picked up her blouse and studied her abdomen in the mirror. She turned and looked at her butt. Satisfied that she had not gained any weight since the morning or the day before, or the week before that, even, she went to the kitchen and prepared three boiled eggs and steamed broccoli. Her stomach rumbled, but despite her hunger she knew that with the first bite she would want to vomit. She prepared her food, and when it was done, she sat down at the table to eat it. The first few bites of hard-boiled egg were a struggle, and she had to wash them down with coffee. After she got through the eggs, she ate her broccoli with less difficulty. Tamales would have gone so much better with coffee, she thought, then pushed the thought away with a shake of her head. When she finished, she drank another cup of coffee. Caffeine was an accelerator, a great metabolism booster.

Her cell phone rang and the caller ID said "Felix".

 "Hello darling."

"Juliaaaaaa... I'm still feeling our session from last night, babe. You were so deliciously wet. That masseuse must have done a great job"

"Oh yes, she did. Believe me, she did a super job."

"I can take lunch at four and we can have a quickie, what do you say?"

Julia smiled and laughed. "You are shameless!"

"Is that a yes though?"

"You know it is. You're terrible."

"I am. That's why you love me. See you, babe!"

Julia closed the cell phone. Felix was an insatiable lover, and anytime that she had just been with a woman, he would be even worse. They had been together that night of the massage, and again in the morning, and now he wanted a "quickie" in the afternoon. She was still sore but she knew that she could make him come quickly just by talking to him about her "massage". What she didn't want to do is deny him and then have him come home later smelling of another woman, which had happened a few times in the past after having rejected his sexual advances.

Chocolate. A Magnum ice cream. It popped into her mind, and she felt like an addict craving for heroin. With almonds. It was right around the corner at the little store, just a few steps away. She downed a full glass of water hoping that it would fill her up enough that the craving would subside, but it didn't. Just one ice cream won't kill you, she thought, and she started for the door. She stopped and turned back, and opened the refrigerator to get out a nonfat yogurt. She grabbed a spoon and ate it slowly, trying to savor every bite, imagining that it was the ice cream bar. She finished it and still felt unsatisfied, and now she felt guilty, too, for having eaten her yogurt before it was time. In two hours, instead of the delicious yogurt, she would have to force herself to eat another hardboiled egg. Tears ran down Julia's face, and she felt sick to her stomach. She went to her bedroom, mounted the exercise bike and pedaled frantically, eager to burn off any excess ghost calories she might have taken in because of her ice cream bar thoughts.

After twenty minutes, Julia dismounted the bike and stared at herself in the mirror again. She took off her clothes and inspected every section of her body. She saw a bit of cellulite on her butt and her thighs, and she was certain that she could see the beginnings of love handles forming. Disgusted, Julia let out a sigh of self-loathing and went to her bathroom to shower. She had never been so self-conscious until shortly after she had married Felix. They had been together just for a few months when he started to come home late at night smelling of perfume. It had been a perfume that she had smelled somewhere before. When she started going to the gym with Felix, she smelt the perfume again, this time not on him, and she remembered wondering why his gym clothes often smelled of this same fragrance, when it all finally made sense to her. She saw Felix smile at the gym woman that smelled of the same fragrance. That woman had a perfect body and Julia was just a twig in comparison.

She was horrified by the way the other woman looked at Felix, and the way they greeted each other at the gym in an all too familiar way. Eventually she went into a jealous rage, followed by a long bout of depression. This resulted in the couple having to change gyms and Julia's newfound obsession with her body. Her marriage was all she had. She had not even completed high school when she married Felix, and by the way she had struggled in school there had been little doubt that she would not ever have finished school anyway. Julia's entire school career had been about fashion, makeup, and popular boys. Her future had long been set to either to be married or work long hours in a factory for a meager wage. The thought of a divorce had been nearly too much for her, and the only way she thought she could recuperate Felix was by having a better body. A perfect body.

6

Lila was performing oral sex on a sweaty, stinky police captain that had been her client for three years. He always tipped her well and was a nice enough guy. He had gone so far to tell her that she could get out of the business whenever she wanted and marry him. Of course, he had also told Lila that she was the only woman that he could get an erection with. She stifled a laugh and it sounded more like she was choking on his erect dick, which made the Captain squeal with delight. He began to get a little harder as he got closer to coming.

"Oh Lila, I love you! I love you!" He screamed, louder as he came, and Lila stifled her need to laugh. He finished and she smiled sweetly as she pulled his condom. She cleaned off his penis with a baby wipe. He was going on about what a good wife she would make for him, how he would not expect her to do too much; they could have a maid. She smiled and nodded, and told him that he was crazy. He got dressed and paid her a nice tip. She hugged his sweaty body, careful not to breathe while she did, and kissed him on the cheek.

They said goodbye, and the second he exited the motel room she ran to the shower to bathe the stink of the Captain from the hug that she had given him. She had a change of clothes in her purse, and as she got ready, she studied her flaws in the mirror as she always did. She remembered her moments with Julia-her perfect curves and skin, the way she had moaned and trembled when she came. Two weeks had passed, and still she had not heard from Julia. She probably wouldn't. Lila put her high heels back on, fastening the black straps just above her perfectly shaped ankles. At least age had not changed that. She gave herself another once-over in the mirror, straightening out her short, black and red dress. Her thong was the same color of red as the red in her dress, and she put on a ribbon around her neck, red as well. Her cell phone rang.

"Hello?"

"Hi there. A few weeks ago, I had you give a massage to my wife, do you remember me?"

"Yes, of course I remember you and your beautiful wife." Her heart raced.

"Yes, that's us. So, I'd like to get your services again, but privately. I'd like to watch."

Her throat became dry and she swallowed. "Yes, of course, no problem."

"How much for the service? I won't be joining in, just watching."

She thought for a moment. She almost would have done it for free. She needed to charge him for watching, though. "Eighty dollars."

He was quiet for a moment. She almost asked if it was too much before he spoke but he agreed to the price and they set the time. She would see Julia again today. He would call her with the motel and room number later. He wanted her to use toys, too. She was elated. She rushed home to make herself up, fix her hair, and find the expensive perfume the Captain had given to her on her last birthday. The idea of her mounting Julia and penetrating her with a strap on made her so wet that she had to change her thong. She received a call from a number she recognized to be from another regular and ignored it. She didn't want to miss the call from Julia's husband.

She nervously smoked while waiting, stepping outside of her apartment so that the smoke wouldn't penetrate her clothes. She would have to take some mouthwash because she didn't want Julia to smell the smoke on her breath. She paced and smoked again. Her phone rang. It was Julia's husband.

7

Julia sat on the bed, nervous anticipation manifesting itself as butterflies in her stomach. Felix stood, visibly nervous too, and paced from one side of the motel room to the other. Juarez had many motels, from those that charged by the hour to fancy ones that cost over a hundred dollars a night; and with as much competition as there was in that city a thirty-dollar hotel room was perfect- clean, king size bed, with its own built-in garage for privacy. Julia saw her image staring down at herself from the mirror positioned above the bed. It was something she never cared for, not really wanting to see herself having sex. That was more for men like Felix that enjoyed seeing themselves as a porn star. She smiled at Felix, and he smiled back and they waited, both with their own sexual expectations on their minds. She wondered if this time around would be even better than the last. Felix kept looking out the window. Julia turned the television channel from the porn station that had already been on when they arrived to a soap opera that she liked. Felix continued to stare impatiently at the parking lot through a crack in the curtains that he kept open with his middle finger.

"Soap operas? Really? Put the porn back on. Get us both in the mood."

Julia frowned and obeyed. *More like get you in the mood.*

Nearly an hour had passed since Felix had called Lila with the name of the motel and the phone number when she arrived. Felix answered the door and they greeted one another with a slight hug and kiss on the cheek, and Lila excused herself for taking so long; she had been clear across the city when he called. Felix told her that it was okay, and then Lila greeted Julia by climbing onto the bed simultaneously kicking off her high heels and giving Julia a tender kiss on the cheek, very close to her mouth. Julia was already feeling moist. They made some small talk, Julia talking about her family in Guadalajara and Lila hers in Chihuahua- Felix looked bored and frustrated- until finally Lila was undressing Julia, kissing her neck while she did.

Julia had three sensitive spots: her neck, back, and feet. She became wetter, and her nipples immediately hardened when Lila began to kiss them affectionately. She lowered, pausing at her belly button, kissing and licking her lower stomach until she lowered down to her clitoris, kissing all around her already moist vaginal lips, kissing her inner thighs, and then finally her clitoris. She stroked her lips with her tongue, fluttering it around the opening, then hardening her tongue she thrust it in and out of her pussy. Julia had a tiny orgasm and Lila continued, working back to Julia's clitoris, and she came again, hard and full, waves of energy coursing through her entire body. Lila had forgotten about Felix until she heard him moan as he jacked-off.

Julia's nipples were steel points. Lila continued to kiss and lick her clitoris, gently, and before she felt another wave coming on, Lila started to work her clitoris between her forefinger and her thumb. Julia came again, harder and louder than before.

Lila was ready to continue but Felix interrupted. Julia looked like she too had forgotten about him and she blushed guiltily.

"Time for the toys, ladies, what do you think?" He held a pink strap on and handed it to Lila who looked to Julia for approval and she nodded. Lila looked embarrassed.

"I really am not sure how to put this on." Felix studied the apparatus for a moment, and then helped her. Lila smiled and began to kiss and lick Julia's clitoris again, making her wetter yet. She did not need any lubricant, something Felix also had brought along, and she opened Julia's legs a bit wider and penetrated her gently, thrusting slowly in and out, her breasts moving rhythmically with her pelvis as she did. Julia wrapped her legs around Lila's waist and together they moved more and more rapidly, frantically until Julia came. Lila didn't stop her rhythmic pulsating thrusts and Julia came once again; each orgasm magically stronger than her last.

Julia looked over at Felix. He was undressed, his cock in his hands, eyes wide- he looked like a crazed pervert. She smiled at him, feeling guilty for the extreme pleasure she had felt with this woman. He looked terribly pleased. He smiled back. Lila looked ready to continue, but Felix was too hot and he mounted Julia and had Lila rub Julia's clitoris while he penetrated her, his member harder and longer than the toy, almost hurting her in the process, a good hurt, pleasurable. She came again, Lila's fingers and Felix's cock a wild combination.

Felix kissed her passionately and went to the shower.

Lila turned to Julia. "Did you enjoy it, sweetheart?"

"Oh yes. I did. I really did." She looked at Lila while she said it.

Lila smiled. "Good. I really like you. Truly. You are so beautiful."

Julia felt the blood rush to her ears and cheeks. Lila noticed, and whispered, "If you ever want to see me, alone, just you and I, just call me. Do you still have my number?" Julia nodded. "And don't worry, I won't charge you. Just keep it between us, okay?" Julia nodded again and Lila kissed her, deliciously. They heard the shower turn off and Lila got dressed.

Felix exited the bathroom wrapped in a towel, his strong chest and shoulders gleaming. He handed Lila folded up money which she took and put into her purse without counting it. They all said goodbye and Lila left. Felix kissed Julia passionately and got hard again. He wanted more, so Julia obliged, but this time his hardness hurt more than it was pleasurable, and she told him that and after two or three more thrusts just to make sure, he dismounted. She finished him off with her mouth and Felix was satisfied. Julia took a shower, and replayed the incredible sex that she had just experienced. Never had she had such powerful orgasms, certainly not with the other ladies that she had been with and never with her husband. And she sure as hell had never had so many orgasms at once. She smiled.

8

Lila was smiling all night. She had even smiled as she fucked the smelly, dirty pig gringo that had chosen her over the younger ladies because he wanted someone with "experience". Julia was in her head, her essence still on her lips and the feel of her skin on her fingertips. It didn't matter what she had to endure this evening because she knew that she had made Julia very happy.

Her nipples had been so hard, her body responding to Lila's touch immediately, and she had been so wet. The chemistry was there, and Lila had made Julia orgasm so intensely she had actually left the bed soaking with her ejaculations. Lila had made many women happy over the years, but never as intensely. But what really had her smiling was the phone call that she had received about two hours after she had left the hotel room.

"Lila?"

"Yesss." She said the word like she was out of breath, Julia's call taking her by surprise.

"I just wanted to tell you, well, I'm not sure how to say it."

"Just say it, and don't worry. We'll figure it out later if it doesn't make sense."

"Well, it's just that I've never felt the way I felt like, you know, when we were together. It was-unbelievable. That was the best - sex- I've ever had."

Lila felt the blood rush to her head with the excitement of hearing this beautiful goddess tell her that she had been the best lover ever.

"I've had many orgasms and sex has never been bad with Felix, but this, well, you, you took me where no one ever has. I've never been so turned on and the orgasms were so intense, so powerful, I just wanted you to know that. Thank you."

"Julia, there's no need to thank me. I enjoyed every minute I had with you. You are a beautiful woman, and I am lucky that I got to be with you. And if you ever decide you want to see me, alone, just you and I, just let me know. Not for pay."

Both Julia and Lila were silent for a moment. Lila began to worry that she had been too forward when Julia finally spoke.

"Okay. I would like that. Can I call you again?"

"Please do. Anytime."

The thought of being alone with Julia made her body shudder. She wanted to make it special, with candles and flowers and just really make love to Julia. And as impractical and terrible as it was, she realized that she was falling for her. There was no denying it. Lila had never before felt quite this way about anyone, and she never had believed in love at first sight until now.

She returned to the bar area and sat at a table, lost in her thoughts. A hand on her shoulder brought her back to the Pink Lady.

"Hey, can I buy you a drink?"

Lila smiled and nodded and turned around to see her pudgy police captain. What was he doing there? He had only gone to the Pink Lady on a few occasions when they first had met. She hugged him, in such a good mood that she was genuinely happy to see the man. He smiled and sat down at the table with her and ordered them drinks.

She looked inquisitively at him and waited for his response. "I just wanted to see you. I needed to see you."

"Captain, you know that we can go out whenever you want, as long as you give me some advance notice."

"I know, but I didn't feel like waiting. What's the difference, really, here or another bar? A bar is a bar, here, and in China."

"Sure, you know I don't mind, but you have to be buying me drinks, that's all. I hate to see you spend your money like that."

"Not to worry. I just got moved to a different sector and it has been going well for me."

"Oh, congratulations!"

"There have been a lot of changes in the department. I have done my best to align myself with the right people. The money is steady."

The captain obviously wanted Lila to know that he was a good catch. Money and stability. Lila didn't want to know the details of this money or who he had aligned himself with. A policeman in Juarez was corrupt. It was a fact of life in this city, like potholes in the streets and junkies begging on the street corners. All that ever changed in Juarez was who was handing out the money and to whom while everyone else avoided the potholes.

9

Julia sat at the edge of her bed, the television set in the corner on. She stared at it, but was not really watching. Her mind was back in the motel room replaying the entire sexual scene over again. Felix had asked her later if she had liked it, and she had blushed and simply said yes, but her real answer was that it had been the greatest sex of her life. And she wanted to see Lila again. A week had passed since the motel experience. She would call her again, and this time set up a time and day to see each other.

"Lila?"

"Yes. Julia?"

"I want to see you again."

"When?"

"Tomorrow? Around noon?"

"Where?"

"Can you come to my house?"

"Will your husband be there?"

"Not this time."

"Is it trouble if he shows up?"

"He's in court in Chihuahua tomorrow and the next day. He won't be back until Friday."

"Okay. How do I get there?"

Julia was ecstatic. She explained in detail directions to her house, and they ended up talking for three hours before they finally said goodbye. She reclined on the bed and imagined Lila making love to her on their king size bed. Her nipples hardened and she was wet. She pulled a vibrator from under the pillow, unzipped her shorts and lowered her panties to expose her clitoris.

She turned the vibrator on and moved it slowly around her clit and fantasized about Lila until she came. Lila's touch was expert, and Julia's body responded to her in ways that it never had before. She remembered her tongue and her suctioning, and she came again. She put away the vibrator and cleaned herself with a vaginal wipe. Felix would have loved to have seen her masturbating, or even to hear about it, but she was going to keep this one to herself. She was going to cheat on him, for the first time without his knowledge, and that excited her, too. She had to keep how badly she wanted Lila from him if she was to keep him from being suspicious.

Felix showed up after seven and she had dinner ready, but he was hungrier for her than for food, and he kissed her passionately, pulling down her panties and shorts in one movement. He pulled his pants down and Julia grabbed his bulging penis, caressing it from outside his underwear. He moaned as she pulled down his boxers. His member sprang out, seemingly reveling in its newfound freedom, and Felix turned Julia around while motioning for her to grab the table. She was still excited from her earlier fantasies, and his animal passion further incited her as she obeyed his commands. He pulled his dick out and penetrated her, simultaneously licking the back of her neck and nibbling on her perfectly shaped back. Julia moaned, partially in pain from his huge, hard dick and also from the intensity of the moment. He manipulated her clitoris with his right hand and pinched her nipples with his left, lightly at first, increasing intensity as he thrusted deep inside her. When she felt him coming inside her, she came with him. Their bodies tensed up and they screamed in animalistic fervor. Finished, he kissed her lips, pulled up his pants and sat down at the table so that she could serve him dinner.

Julia served the chicken breasts and steamed broccoli that she had made earlier. They ate their dinner with salsa and two corn tortillas each. The chicken breasts had marinated in white wine, parsley, celery salt, pepper and olive oil overnight. She had squeezed lime onto the breasts as she sautéed them. She missed eating flautas, enchiladas, tamales, and posole, but there was no going back from this diet. Her cellulite had nearly been eliminated since she had gone on the diet. While she was considering the hated cellulite, Felix was talking about work, and she nodded, smiled when he smiled, and ultimately had no idea as to what he had been talking about for the last forty minutes. She studied her toes, and decided that she needed to have a pedicure before her appointment with Lila and decided to call her in the morning and set it for later so she could ensure that she looked her absolute best. Felix was staring at her and had quit talking.

"I'm sorry, dear. I was thinking about getting a pedicure. I missed what you just said."

Felix laughed and smiled. "Not to worry. Just boring shop talk. Let's get ready for the gym."

It had been only a few occasions in their five years of marriage that he had gotten angry with her, and it scared her to death when he did. Luckily, he was very patient, and usually she could keep him from angering by having sex with him, which was hardly ever unpleasant. All things considered, he was really easy to please.

Feed him and fuck him, and Felix was a happy man.

After a heavy leg workout at the gym and a hot shower, the insatiable Felix wanted her again, but she was beat and asked if he would settle for a helping hand. He agreed, so she took care of him, whispering in his ear and kissing him as she did. He kissed her goodnight and fell immediately asleep. She thought of Lila as she drifted off and dreamed of her sweet, tender kisses.

Felix suspected that Julia was up to something.

Normally she was always worried about how soon he would get back from wherever he would leave town for, hating to be alone, but this time she almost seemed disappointed that he would only be gone overnight. Felix overheard her scheduling a nail appointment for the morning. While she was in the shower, he had checked her phone for calls and messages, but everything had been cleared, and that was something that Julia did not normally do. Her behavior overall was strange, nervous, and suspicious. Years of dealing with guilty people made Felix particularly in tune to those types of behaviors.

Court in the capital city of Chihuahua was as usually drawn out and boring as ever. All Felix could think of was what Julia might be up to. At lunch he called a friend affectionately known as Nacho and asked him to watch the house and follow Julia.

He received a text at about two in the afternoon from Nacho- *blue Explorer arrived, and a lady-friend entered the house.* Felix only knew of one lady that Julia knew with a blue Explorer, and that was Lila. As he pondered the implications of the visit, he became erect and he hoped that he would not have to stand up any time soon. A few hours had passed and he had not received any further text message from Nacho, so Felix sent one—*is she still there?*

Yes.

Felix was still excited, but now he was wondering what they were doing for three hours. When Julia and he had sex, it was always for thirty minutes to an hour. Any longer and she would start to complain.

Everyone in the court was looking at him and he realized he had just been asked a question. He turned red and asked for them to repeat the question. Luckily it was something simple, not requiring him to lie or use any of the cover story that he and his partner would have in place before they attended court. His mind wandered again back to his house and he imagined Julia, her back arched and nipples hard, and Lila between her legs. It was almost too much for him to bear, and luckily the court went to recess for the day. Felix motioned to his partner.

"Let's go, man."

Rafa smiled. "Hungry, huh?"

Felix sneered. "You have no idea." They got into their gray Ram and Felix drove to a massage parlor that he had frequented before.

"What the hell, man?" Rafa looked genuinely distressed.

"Pussy before sandwiches."

"Fuck that! I'm hungry."

"Fine," Felix told Rafa as he got out of the truck, "leave me here and go stuff your face with a torta. Come back in an hour."

Rafa frowned, obviously disappointed. "Fine."

He sped off. Felix shrugged and went into the massage parlor. From outside, it appeared to be like any other office, home to a lawyer or real estate agent. Inside, however, seven beautiful young women lined up to greet Felix so that he could choose one. He chose two.

Even as horny as he was, Felix had trouble getting off due to one of the girls really not being into the other girl. If he asked for a two-girl fantasy, he wanted them to really have fun with each other, even if he was paying for it. The girl that really put the effort in gave him a decent blow job and he finally came after he told the other girl to leave, just making it under the hour he had requested. He tipped the blow job girl, showered and dressed, and exited the room. Rafa was still not there and didn't answer the radio, so Felix chose another girl, a bit on the plump side who had been eyeing him since he had entered and had looked genuinely disappointed when he hadn't picked her. He let her massage him, and enjoyed her telling him how great his body looked and how handsome he was. As he fucked her from behind. She was already wet, but literally gushed as he reached around her belly to rub her clit. When she came, she screamed so loud it made him come too. After he bathed again, Felix left the plump girl showering (she had insisted he take her number down to see her again) and Rafa was waiting in the lobby, and he started laughing as they left.

"Shit Felix, that girl should've paid you!"

"She almost did. You going to get some?"

Rafa shook his head no. "I'm too full. Maybe tonight at the hotel room."

"You really like those surprises, don't you? I never order out unless I'm looking at the menu. That's why I always come to the buffets."

"I know. Remember that time I sent six girls home and that pimp came by to start shit?"

Felix laughed. "How can I forget? When he found out we were cops he nearly shit himself. We sure gave him a good beating. Probably should have capped him."

"And have missed out on all the free pussy we got after? Hell no!"

"Yeah, but I was worried that he would send us some disease-stricken bitch."

"Condoms, Felix. You should use them."

"Compadre, I always use them. Well, almost always. At least the first time."

"Why is it that you're the married one, and you're worse than me?"

"Experience, my boy. Many years of perversion and experience."

Felix picked up a salad to go and drove back to the hotel room. He ate his salad, changed into shorts and went to the hotel gym. It was a typical hotel gym, lacking in free weights, but he hit the nautilus machine as hard as he could and still got a great pump. He went back to his room, and a do not disturb sign was on the door. Rafa was busy. His cell phone buzzed that a new text message had arrived.

Explorer woman just left. Long hug at the door and they kissed. Now Felix was pissed. Nacho would know that Julia was into girls, although he knew better than to say anything; everyone that knew Felix knew that his sadism had no limits. Worse yet, what if a neighbor had seen, he thought. He never expected for Julia to have a public display of affection with anyone but him, and while he enjoyed her being bisexual privately, he sure didn't want the whole neighborhood to know.

Just the same, he had another hard on again as he sent a message back to Nacho- *abort the mission.*

Want me to off the Explorer lady?

It was funny that Nacho immediately understood the implications of the situation; he was ready to kill her and all Felix had to do was text a yes back. This was true power, life or death at the whim of a cell phone message. Felix paused, thinking that maybe it wouldn't be such a bad idea, but changed his mind because he really wanted to see them together again. He was betting that now their chemistry would be even hotter. He texted Nacho "no" and went to the hotel bar. He rarely drank since alcohol was such a detriment to his workouts and diet, but he had a strange feeling of jealousy that he had never experienced before, and he really wanted to drown it. He started with a scotch- Chivas and mineral water on the rocks. A few hours had passed and Felix's cell rang. It was Julia.

"Hey there."

"Hey there yourself. Felix, have you been drinking?"

"Have I."

"That's not like you, love. What's going on?"

"Nothing." Felix hung up. Julia called back a few times, but Felix had shut off his phone.

Julia must have contacted Rafa because he showed up a few minutes later. Felix was barely able to stand. He helped him to the room and into bed. Felix passed out, forgetting all about Julia's phone call. When he awoke at three in the morning, he had several texts and a few voicemails from her. His head was throbbing and his mouth was dry. He called her.

"Hello?"

"You're not asleep yet?"

"I couldn't. I was worried about you."

"Sorry. I had a few drinks at the bar and before I knew it was passed out in my bed."

"Yeah, I know. Don't you remember hanging up on me?"

"No. Baby, I'm sorry, I was really drunk."

"Yes, I figured that. No worries, at least you are sleeping by yourself, I hope?"

Felix sighed. "Rafa is in the other bed."

"You know what I mean."

"I do. I was drunk. Too drunk to do anything else even if I had wanted to."

"Fine. Are you hungover?"

"Very."

"Good. Serves you right."

"Hey! No need to be mean. I'm glad you are okay." Felix was careful with what he said and his voice intonation, not wanting to let on that he knew what she had done.

"I'm glad you are okay, too. You better get some sleep. What time do you have court?"

"Not until nine. But you're right. I need to get over this hangover before that. I love you."

"Me too."

Felix hung up and got his shoes on. He'd have to make a run for a convenience store for something to hydrate himself. He stopped at a local OXXO. The clerk had a look of anguish that he could not contain and Felix realized that he was being robbed. *Just my luck*, Felix thought, *hungover and then this shit*. He pulled out his nine mil and walked carefully around the Ram, putting the engine block between him and the suspect. The suspect saw and seemed to recognize that the grey Ram and Felix's demeanor meant that Felix was the police. The suspect dropped his gun, obviously not ready to shoot it out. Felix had him get down on his knees and he cuffed him with some flex cuffs. He bought some Gatorade and downed it. Then he proceeded to kick the man in the chest and back and wherever his feet landed. The clerk turned away.

"Hey! This is for you! This asshole had a gun pointed at you and now you can't watch me kick the shit out of him? What if he had capped you? Would you be so worried about me mistreating him then?"

The clerk shook his head, and turned to watch as Felix continued to pummel the would-be robber, his sadistic smile wide despite the hangover. He had the clerk help him pick up the man after he had passed out from the beating and put him in the back of the pickup. He then drove to a street corner a few blocks away and left the man there. He really didn't feel like doing paperwork with the headache he had.

Besides, he thought, *this asshole will think twice before robbing another store.*

11

Julia blushed while on the phone with Lila. "When can I see you again?"

"Whenever you want."

"Seriously?"

"Yes. I told you the other day- I'm really into you. More than I've ever been into anyone." Lila bit her tongue after saying that- *don't say too much, you might scare her off.*

"That means a lot to me. I can't wait to see you again. Felix has court again in a week."

Lila was relieved that Julia hadn't been put off by her slip of the tongue.

"Okay. I'll be there. Just call me the day before."

"Okay."

Lila hung up the cell and puffed on her cigarette. Julia had called her five times since they had been together at Julia's house, and had sent twenty text messages. Lila had pulled out all the stops the day that she was alone with Julia. She obviously had done a good job. Julia had caused quite an impression on her as well. She had been so wet, so hot, and had become very reciprocal as their intimacy had progressed that day. Her thoughts were interrupted when her cell rang. The caller

ID identified the caller as "cap" for her captain in the police force. He was calling and texting more often, and was continuously harassing her to marry him, or at least move in with him.

"Hello lover."

"Lila, where are you?"

"My house. Why?"

"Can I see you?"

"You know I have to work tonight."

"Call in sick."

"I can't afford to. They might not let me work when I want to later."

"You know you don't have to work at all. I can take care of you. My new position has been very lucrative."

"Don't start."

"I'll pay you for your time."

"I don't mind taking your money, Gordito, but you know I don't like to take advantage of you."

"That's what I love about you. You aren't. I want to see you and I don't care what it costs. It's only money and I can't take it with me, now, can I? Are we going to argue, or are we going to go out?"

"Pick me up at the Pink Lady and pay the fee for me to leave. That way I don't lose my job, okay?"

"Will do."

Lila was actually relieved that the Captain was going to pick her up, and that she wouldn't have to hustle drinks and fucks all night. It was preferable going on a date with him; not a lot more preferable, but preferable just the same. Lila went through the usual motions of fixing her face, arranging her outfit, and doing her hair, but her mind was on Julia. Especially those amazing kisses.

Julia was an excellent kisser, the best she had ever kissed, man or woman. She drove to the Pink Lady, arriving abruptly, her brain on autopilot; she didn't even recall the trip. She shrugged and got out, and walked to the back entrance of the Pink Lady. The door was guarded by a chubby brute named Pito, and they all made fun of him because pito was also another way to say penis-the man's head really did resemble the head of a penis, which made his nickname even funnier. His real name was an awful mouthful, Agapito. Lila's Captain showed up and paid the "exit" fee. Lila made a call to her babysitter that she needed her all night. Lila would give him a true girlfriend experience and after as long as they had known each other it was easy to do. Despite his "shortcomings", the captain was the closest thing that she had to a friend. By the time they had danced, ate and drank, the Captain was too drunk to get it up and he fell asleep beside her in the motel bed. Lila lit a cigarette, took a long, thoughtful drag, slowly releasing the smoke out of her mouth and nostrils. The Captain had told her that he loved her several times throughout the course of the evening, and Lila wondered if perhaps it would be nicer of her to go ahead and break it off with him before things got more out of hand. He began to snore loudly and she poked him in the ribs until he stopped. She finished her cigarette and fell asleep, Julia in her thoughts and then in her dreams.

The Captain was already awake when Lila got up, and he drove her to her apartment. He had wanted to take her to breakfast but she had to get back before her girls woke up so that she could make them breakfast. She made them pancakes, and soon the smell must have awoken them because they ran to the kitchen and hugged her. Carmen sat down and devoured the pancakes on her plate and started eyeing Yamileth's, too.

"Hey, Carmencita, I can make you more. You know your sister eats like a bird, but leave hers alone."

"Okay, Mami."

Lila got up from the table and made a few more pancakes. She drank her coffee and was craving a cigarette, but ignored the craving; she'd wait until the girls were done and go outside. Carmen talked about school and her teacher and the movie they saw the night before with the babysitter and Yamileth, the quieter of the two, occasionally chimed in. Lila was nearly dizzy with all of Carmen's talking, but she understood the girl's need for her mother's attention, so she smiled and nodded and asked her questions about the movie. She asked Yamileth about school, and had a difficult time getting her to talk, but finally she opened up when Lila asked about her most recent drawings and she retrieved them from her room to show her. Yamileth was an excellent artist even at her age, and

Lila often bought her special pencils and paper so that she could draw.

"Mami!" Carmen could no longer contain herself while Yamileth showed them her artwork. "Can we please go to the park today? Say yes! Please?"

Lila smiled and nodded wearily. Sunday was the only day they had to spend together without her having to work or the girls going to school. After the park, she would have to take them shopping for some new school uniforms and school supplies, and later for groceries. There would be no rest for her, but she cherished her day with the girls and would do everything to make it an amazing day for them. Her mind wandered back to Julia and she texted her.

When can I see you again? Sorry couldn't wait.

It was over an hour before Lila received a text back. She was already certain that her brief but intense affair was over when her cell phone buzzed.

Tuesday.

12

"I look in the mirror and all I see are my wrinkles, breasts starting to sag, and the lines of expression. It is awful getting old." Lila told Julia. Her head was on Julia's naked breast and her black hair flowed over Julia's chest, a sort of see-through shawl.

Julia frowned at what Lila had said. "That's crazy. You're not old. You're mature. Like a fine wine."

Lila laughed and smiled, and hugged Julia. They kissed. Lila looked at Julia directly into her emerald eyes. "You are the most beautiful woman in the world. I'm crazy about you."

"And I adore you, cielito. Are you hungry? I can make you something to eat."

"Only if you're going to eat too."

Julia pondered the idea of eating. A fruit salad would be in order after having sweated the last few hours with Lila. "Okay. You like fruit salad?"

"As long as it doesn't have banana or grapefruit."

"Neither. Strawberries, pineapple, apple, papaya, cottage cheese and pecans."

"Mmm. Sounds delicious. Don't you eat anything that's not healthy Julia?"

Julia frowned, then laughed. "Very rarely. If I do, it's tamales. I love tamales."

Lila smiled. "One day we'll have to have coffee and tamales."

"Shut up already! You'll ruin my diet."

The two women got dressed and walked down the stairs. Julia wore a short, white sundress, and Lila had a cute pair of jeans shorts. She wore leather sandals with white floral tops, and Lila wore red platform sandals to match her halter top. Julia admired Lila's long, sender legs as they walked down the stairs to the kitchen. Lila turned around at the bottom of the stairs, and kissed Julia, passionately, who responded accordingly. Julia smiled. "Lila, you're making me wet again!"

"I can take care of that."

Lila guided Julia to the kitchen counter, noting that it was impeccably clean. Julia hopped up and opened her legs to expose her wet pussy, and Lila began kissing and licking her until Julia came in her mouth. Julia got down from the counter, and kissed Lila. "Thank you." She whispered.

"You are very welcome. A snack before the meal."

Julia laughed while she prepared the fruit salad from the fresh fruits that she kept in her fridge. They sat down at the small kitchen table in the dining room, ate and talked about everything and nothing, from clothes to sex to the lack of security in Juarez. Julia could never had talked to Felix the way she did with Lila. Both because he didn't really listen to her, or she to him, and in the end the only things they had in common was working out and sex. The ladies spent hours together and Julia was sad to see Lila leave, but she was relieved when she finally did go because Felix was due to be home any minute.

Rafa hit a suspect hard in the jaw. He had a roll of pesos in his fist, and when he hit the man, the jaw made a crunching sound that made Rafa cringe. He looked over at Felix. Felix sat on another chair in the interrogation room, a smile on his face that reminded Rafa of the Cheshire cat. He also had a hard on that was impossible not to notice.

"What the fuck, Felix?" He said pointing at his dick.

"Hey, don't worry man, you're not my type! I just really enjoy a good beating."

"Fuck, you're crazy man. Glad you are on my side. You are on my side, right?"

"Until death do us part, fucker." Felix made a sign with his hands like someone shooting with an AK-47.

"Good." He turned back to the suspect and furrowed his thick brow. "What the fuck are you looking at?" He hit him in the eye which bleed and swelled up immediately. Felix giggled. Rafa switched the roll of coins to his other hand and hit the suspect with his left hand in the liver.

The man doubled over as much as was physically possible considering that he was tied up to an office chair. "Want to make the pain stop?" Rafa asked the man. He nodded emphatically that he did. Felix got up from his chair and grabbed the man, chair and all, moving him to a table that was in the middle of the stark, gray room. A paper and pen were in front of him.

"First, you'll sign this confession," Felix said while banging his index finger onto the paper, "then you will memorize it. When the reporters get here, you will recite it word for word to them. If you forget a piece of it or deviate in any way,", Felix pulled out a photo of the suspect alongside his wife and kids, "I'll make what my partner did to you just now seem pleasurable compared to what I will do to them."

The suspect cringed and shook his head, and motioned that he would sign the paper. Rafa took off the cuffs and let the man sign the confession that they had written saying he had murdered several young women and later buried them in the desert. He picked up the confession and began to go over it. Felix and Rafa smiled because they had just "resolved" yet another case. It would also appease the activists and media for at least a little while.

Felix wanted to catch Julia in the act with the puta and then fuck them both, hard. After the suspect was put back into the holding cell, Felix rushed home. He was disappointed when he arrived and found Julia alone, madly pedaling on the exercise bike. She was sweeter than ever to him, even making him his favorite dinner: enchiladas suizas. That night she sucked him to completion, and when he tried to reciprocate, she told him that she was fine and that she was dead from all the exercise she had done. All of this perturbed Felix, and he barely slept. He needed to install the surveillance system he had bought and had hidden in a box in their closet a few days earlier. *I'll send her to the grocery store tomorrow and do it then.* He finally slept. His dreams were full of sex and violence. Just the way he liked them to be.

"Babe, when are you going to the store?"

"I thought we were going together since today is your day off."

"I really can't. I need to get some paperwork done." Julia frowned.

"You have to go to the office?"

"Not today. I have work to do here at the house." Felix pulled out a bundle of American hundred-dollar bills and handed two to Julia. "Why don't you hit the mall and buy yourself some shoes, or bras, or whatever, and then go grocery shopping."

"Fine. You had me at shoes and bras."

"By the time you get back I should be done."

Julia studied Felix's face, suspicious. He displayed no emotion and finished his breakfast while she stared at him. She nodded, apparently satisfied that he had no ulterior motives. After breakfast, she showered, dressed, and left for the store.

Felix waited about twenty minutes after Julia had left to take out the system. He had bought a pinhole camera and drilled a hole in the wall from the closet after cutting a piece of the sheetrock out. It gave him a perfect view of the bed from the side. He drilled another hole for a special microphone so sensitive that it could pick up a pin dropping from five meters distance. He connected the wires to the remote access device and connected the device to a set of wires he had pulled from the wall. When he was finished, he covered the hole he had made by replacing the sheetrock, applying mesh tape and a sealing compound. He then painted the spot, and he was quite impressed with his work when he finished. He installed the software into his laptop and took control of the remote device. The picture was perfect. He sat on the bed and made quiet, moaning sounds and recorded it. He played it back and it was louder than the original sound he had made. He would be able to see and hear absolutely everything that occurred on this bed, right from his laptop. He was erect and angry, pissed and horny at the same time.

13

Felix sat in the motel room that he had rented to watch Julia with her prostitute girlfriend. He had a puta with him as well, and his plan was for her to blow him while he watched his wife. His stomach was in disarray due to his nerves, but he was sure he could still have a good erection once the action got started.

"How long before the show, honey?" Her face was not very pretty, but her body was incredible. *Body of temptation with a face of regret.*

"Not sure. You going to watch too?"

"You said it is two girls fucking live, right?"

"Yup."

"Yeah, why not, sounds sexy. Will it be much longer?"

"Hey! I'm paying you by the hour, right?"

"Well, yeah. Can I watch TV while we wait though?"

"Yeah, sure, whatever." He waived his hand to show his indifference and continued to monitor the laptop connection. Julia had been in and out a few times, had changed outfits three different occasions, apparently not happy with the first two, and had sat in front of the mirror for what had felt like an eternity to Felix plucking her eyebrows and fixing her hair and makeup. When Lila and Julia finally appeared on the camera together and on the bed, Felix's nerves worsened and he had to hit the bathroom.

"Watch them and tell me what's going on while I'm on the toilet!"

"Okay, fine."

Felix sat down on the toilet, "What are they doing?"

"Nothing, just talking."

"No kissing or touching?"

"Well, they are holding hands."

"Okay. Let me know if something else happens."

"I will."

Felix finished up, washed his hands, and hurried back to the bed. He had his laptop on top of a dresser that was directly in front of the queen size in the middle of the room and the girl scooted over as he sat down. She began to unzip his pants and he waived her off. "Not yet, wait until I tell you."

The girl shook her head and shrugged and went back to viewing the "live show". The two women on the screen were locked in a passionate embrace, now naked and kissing each other. The older woman began to kiss the younger woman's neck, moving down to her breasts and flat stomach, then Julia gently pushed her down to her pussy. She opened up the younger woman's legs and kneeled down on the floor and began to suck and lick her. The popping sound was loud as she used her lips to suction the other woman's clit. She moved her tongue in and out of Julia's pussy, and the girl that Felix had hired began to play with herself.

She looked over at him, and now he was naked and fully erect. She decided that it was a good moment to start. She caressed his member with her fingertips, which apparently startled him at first, as if he had forgotten that she was there, and he then relaxed as she used her mouth instead of her hands.

"Oh God, wait, wait just a second."

She stopped. She was good at what she did, and the "live show" apparently was also good. She looked at the laptop screen while she waited for him to let her do her job again, and the younger woman was moving her hips rhythmically with the other woman's tongue thrusting in and out of her. Then the older woman began to suck and finger her until the younger woman orgasmed, long and hard, biting her lower lip as she did, her back arched and her muscular body tense. The other woman continued to suck and move her finger in and out, even after the orgasm was over until once again the younger woman came, just as long and just as hard. She forgot about Felix, and he apparently had forgotten about her too. Then the two women on the screen laid side by side, kissing and talking.

"Oh Lord, will they ever get back to business? Why do fucking chicks talk so damn much?"

The girl did not answer. She assumed the question was rhetorical. After about twenty minutes the women began kissing each other intensely. They began to scissor. Felix's hooker touched herself, her pussy moist, and she moved Felix towards her, put a condom on him so that he could penetrate her, which he did. He was very well-endowed and with the noise the women were making on the computer, and the occasional glimpse she got, she was able to come easily. Felix also came, and then the two sat on the bed and watched the rest of the function.

The older woman was using a vibrator on the younger girl. She also had a strap-on, and the younger woman told her to mount her before she came again and the older woman obeyed. They rocked together and the younger woman wrapped her legs around the older woman's back and she came again, her moan louder than before. Once again, the older woman didn't miss a beat and the younger woman came again. "I love you, Julia."

"I love you too."

Felix felt the blood in his veins hot and it rose to his face. He grabbed his pants from the dresser and pulled out a hundred and gave it to the girl.

"Go. Now."

"Oh, can't I finish the show? It's just getting interesting."

"Get the fuck out, now." Felix spoke quietly, but it was more powerful than if he had yelled.

The girl quickly got dressed and left. Felix grabbed his computer and threw it at the wall. It crashed and fell to pieces and he continued with the dresser, kicking it and throwing the pieces at the TV. He ripped the television from the wall. He broke the mirror. He hit the wall with his fists, making bloody holes. He kicked the bed and hurt his foot on the metal. He screamed in rage, and didn't hear the manager knocking at the door until he finally stopped and sat down on the bed.

"What do you want?"

"Is everything all right in there, sir?"

"It's fine! I broke some stuff. I'll pay for the damage. Just leave me alone."

"Sir, I'm afraid I'll need to see the damage now."

Felix pulled his .45 from the holster now on the floor and chambered a round. He opened the door and put the gun to the man's head. The manager broke into a sweat and was frozen in fear.

"I told you I'll pay for it. And don't bother calling the cops. I am one."

He slammed the door shut and sat down again, holding his head in his hands. He never expected this to happen. Before this. Felix had been in charge of her sex, even when it was with other women, but this was different. This was sex like he had never seen her have before, not even with him. And then the love stuff. That was unfathomable for him. He couldn't get his head around how his wife could be in love with someone else, and another woman at that. She had never made those faces or moaned this way with him, and that bothered him, too. It was as if, no matter how impossible it seemed to Felix, that she liked being with the whore more than being with him.

Now he understood why Julia had begun to give him more blow jobs and not want any sex in return. She really did like being with the whore more. He needed to end this. He could off the whore, although he didn't know where she lived. He could follow her from his house the next time she was there, which over the last few weeks had been at least every other day. He would strangle the bitch and dump her body in the desert. No one would worry about another dead whore in Juarez, and then he could get Julia back to loving him. She would hurt for a bit, but eventually she would go back to the way she was; and now, he would definitely not ask her to be with another woman again. No way. He took a shower and got dressed. He stopped at the motel's office on his way out and gave the manager four bills. Felix sped back to his house.

Julia was daydreaming as she did yoga in her bedroom. She thought of Lila, the way she touched and kissed her, the incredible way she felt when they were together. She barely heard Felix when he arrived. She could hear him quietly walking up the steps. Maybe he thought she was not alone. He had been acting very strange of late. Julia took the position of Downward-Facing Dog Pose when Felix grabbed her from behind, his cock fully erect and out of his pants. She winced and fell out of position.

"Felix! What the hell?"

Felix had a hurt look on his face.

"What?"

"Don't be such a pervert!"

Felix shrugged and put his penis in his pants and zipped up, his erection slowly fading. "You used to like me perverted. Now you don't even have sex with me."

"I gave you a blow job just last night."

Julia knew what he meant but feigned ignorance. She had not allowed him inside of her for weeks. His touch no longer excited her the way that Lila's did. She didn't even care if he was screwing other women or not anymore. She had found something so special with Lila that Felix was no longer as important to her, at least not in the same way as before.

Felix scowled. "You know what I mean!"

Julia jumped. Felix had never yelled at her. She had seen how mean he could be, but always with others. She once witnessed a brutal beating he gave to three men just for making a lewd comment in passing about her ass. He had never been mean to her, and in fact, he had always been a real gentleman. Felix saw her reaction, but he didn't stop there. His hands were shaking.

"I know about you and your little whore girlfriend."

"Don't call her that." Felix looked surprised that she didn't deny her relationship and instead defended the other woman.

"Well, that is what she is, you know." He said, sheepishly.

"She might be a prostitute, but she is my best friend, and I care for her very much. Don't ever say that again, Felix."

"Your best friend? When did that happen?"

"You've obviously been spying on me so you know we have been seeing each other. She's really my only friend, besides you."

"Yeah a friend that you fuck all the time. Is she better than me in bed?"

"Please, Felix."

"Just answer me."

"It's different. I can't compare."

"You can."

"Felix-"

"Answer me God damn it!"

"Yes! She's better than you! She makes me feel like I've never felt with anyone! Happy?"

Felix looked at his feet and shuffled them back and forth.

"Not really. Do you love her?"

Julia stared at Felix's feet and didn't answer for a minute.

"Yes, I do."

Felix grabbed some clothes from the closet, stuffed them into a gym bag, and left the house. Julia didn't try to stop him. She sat on the edge of her bed, head in her hands, and sobbed. She texted Lila and told her that now that Felix knew about them, not only would they not be able to see each other for a while, but that Lila should be careful.

14

"Can I see you, Julia?"

"Lila, you know what I texted you the other day. I'm so sorry, but I can't. Not yet."

"I know but I really need to see you. Please."

Julia sighed. She could hear the anguish in her lover's voice. "Okay."

"Can you meet me at Barriga's on Triunfo De La Republica Street?"

"I can be there in thirty minutes."

"Thank you."

Julia took a fast shower and put on jeans, a pink blouse, and matching sandals. She drove as fast as she could through the traffic and got to the restaurant bar Barriga's in less than thirty minutes. Lila was standing outside, waiting for her, smoking a cigarette. Julia really wished she wouldn't smoke. They hugged and kissed each other on the cheek and went in. Julia had texted Felix that she was leaving for a while, but he didn't answer. She hadn't heard from him in two days since they had spoken about her relationship with Lila. A young woman in a miniskirt interrupted her thoughts and showed them to a table. They sat down and ordered Margaritas.

"What's wrong, Lila? And what's with the sunglasses?"

Lila pulled them down revealing her swollen, black eye. Julia gasped.

"That wasn't the worst part. He punched me in the stomach and the kidney. I'm peeing blood."

"Who did?" Julia asked, although she knew the answer.

"Felix. God, Julia, why did you tell him?"

"I didn't have to. He knew. I couldn't hide my feelings for you forever."

Lila nodded her head. "My love, he threatened my life. I think he means it."

Julia was red with anger. "That bastard! I'll kill him if he hurts you again."

"No Julia, you won't. He's dangerous."

Julia shook her head. "And what does that mean? Not see you again?" That would be worse than death."

Lila took Julia's hand. "We wait. Just a while, and then we see each other discreetly. I just wanted to see you this once before we take some time apart."

"What if I leave him?"

Lila smiled at Julia's innocence. "If you do, we still need to wait so that he has time to cool down. And really, Julia, what would we do? I can't support us both."

"I'll work."

"Doing?"

"I don't know-whatever."

Lila smiled. "Darling, work in Juarez is scarce at best, and for women, well, the only thing that really pays decently is what I do. And I doubt that you want to do what I do".

Julia hung her head and shook it. She did not. "We could move to another city."

"I can't. My girls are in school here. Look, don't worry, we will just take some time, let things cool down, and then figure out what to do."

Julia frowned. "You don't love me anymore."

"Don't ever say that. I love you more than ever. I just don't want either of us to get hurt- worse."

"Okay. But I still want you to call and text me. If he's around, I'll keep the cell off."

"Fine, but you need to delete the texts, too."

"I will."

They hugged and left. Julia cried all of the drive home. Felix still wasn't home. Despite her anger, she couldn't say honestly that she felt nothing for him. Her life had revolved around him for years until she met Lila, but she could not let Felix hurt Lila again, or worse. But she also understood his anger, and she pitied him. It was strange having such contrary feelings at the same time.

Felix showed up after about a week. Julia had called and texted. After so many years together she was genuinely worried about him. He had not been back to see Lila again. He knocked on the door and she let him in. His aroma of alcohol, cheap perfume, and cigarettes filled the living area when he arrived, and Julia knew that he had been dealing with the issue like a typical Mexican man, by drinking and whoring. She was glad he was okay, though.

"Want something to eat?"

"Not really."

"How long has it been since you've eaten?"

"Not sure."

"I can tell. You look skinnier. Come on, go take a shower, and I'll fix you an omelet."

"I'd really rather eat something soupy."

Julia smiled. "I'll go around the corner and bring you some birria."

"Okay." Felix went upstairs. Julia walked about a half block to a small restaurant that was on the corner and bought some birria, a kind of soup made of goat and broth, mixed with spices and chile. She asked for extra chile because Felix would want the birria extra spicy to help get rid of his hangover. The birria came with limes, onion, and cabbage on the side. It smelled delicious, but Julia had eaten the whites of three boiled eggs already, and birria had too much fat for her diet. As she walked back to the house, a short, heavy-set neighbor woman stopped her.

"Julia!"

"Hi Iliana. How are you?"

"Good. How are you, though?"

Julia sighed. Iliana had likely noticed that Felix had been gone for a week and wanted to know why so she could spread the gossip. "I'm fine."

"Really? I mean, your husband-"

"Has been gone on business. That's all. Some big court case in Mexico City."

Iliana nodded, plainly wearing the dissatisfaction with Julia's hardly gossip worthy answer on her face.

"I've got to go. Felix's waiting for his breakfast." Julia didn't wait for Iliana to respond and turned and walked to her house. Women like Iliana was the reason why Julia hardly had any lady friends. She entered the house and found Felix sitting at the dining table. She put his food in front of him and made some coffee. Felix ate slowly, rubbing his temple as he did. Julia served them both coffee and sat down with him. He ate without talking, and she did not disturb the silence. She picked up the foam dishes when he finished, and threw them away and sat down again.

"Want something for your headache?"

"No, I'll be fine in a little bit."

"Can we talk?"

"Isn't that what we're doing?"

"You know what I mean."

"I do. Talk then."

"I've thought a lot about this. I think I have a solution that will benefit us all." She paused to look at Felix. He was staring down at the table.

"I'm listening," he said.

"Well, look, I love you and I like the life we have. I love Lila, too, and I'd like to see her occasionally. I have enough love in my heart for both of you. And I really don't want to see this get violent again or hurt anyone. I think I just let things get a little out of hand with her, since it is so new to me and all that. I propose that we continue like before, and, well, you know, we can have as much sex as often as you like, as kinky as you want it. And I will keep what I do with Lila discreet."

Felix stayed silent. Minutes passed by, seeming to Julia like hours. She was about to speak when he looked up at her, the anger in his stare permeating her every cell. "Julia, I have a proposal for you. Stop seeing your puta, and I won't have to kill her".

Julia took a deep breath and swallowed back her fear. "Felix, be reasonable. This is your fault, after all. You got me started!"

"I did. You're right, that's my fault. But I won't let that happen again. And you are not going to have some whore girlfriend while we are married."

"And why not? It isn't like you haven't had girlfriends. And I know you have had a lot more than just one!"

Felix smiled a strange, twisted grin that caused Julia to shiver. "You heard my proposal. Take it or leave it."

Julia calmed herself down by concentrating on her breathing. She had planned for this, just in case he continued his threats. "Felix, I know where all your extra money comes from. I know a lot about it, actually. I even met your boss once, remember? You took me to that party where all of those mafia people were. The Linea. I even found some records of transactions in your files here at home, along with names." She stopped and observed Felix's reaction. She found courage in his apparent surprise and continued. "I made copies so if something happens to me, and especially if something happens to Lila, that information will go to the federal police."

Felix's hands made fists. His face was red. "And just how is that going to happen?"

Julia was frightened, but she couldn't show fear now. She had already gone too far. "Don't worry about how. Just know that as long as nothing happens to either of us, it won't happen."

"Julia, you surprised me. I never thought you would have enough brains to do something like this." Felix got up from the table and went upstairs. He shut the bedroom door behind him. Julia was trembling. She wished she could see Lila. She wished Felix had never found out. She wished so many things that were not going to happen.

15

Felix didn't stop torturing the man they had picked up even after Rafa had told him that he was the wrong guy several times over. The man's eyes were huge with panic. He had a plastic bag over his head and was suffocating. Felix made a tiny hole in the bag where the man's mouth was and his eyes relaxed, just a bit. His breathing was labored, but at least he was getting some oxygen now. Then Felix took the gum that he was chewing out of his mouth and plugged the hole he had made with it, laughing like a child. The man thrashed about, and the piece of gum fell, but the oxygen was still too little and he passed out. Felix ripped the bag off of the man's head. The guy's breath was shallow and labored.

"Partner, how long are we going to do this?"

"That's it. I'm done. Let's go get the right target."

"Now you're talking, partner."

"Just let me take care of this real quick." Felix pulled out his secondary weapon, a nine mil, and shot the man in the head. Rafa was surprised, but decided not to say anything. Something was especially wrong with Felix, and he had noticed a particularly vicious trend over the last few weeks, even for Felix. He had just murdered a man that had nothing to do with the task that they had been given. Talking to Felix like this might be hazardous even for Rafa.

They left the abandoned house that they had chosen to torture the guy, and Felix drove them back to the neighborhood where they had picked him up. After driving around for a few hours, scouring the area, they finally found the right target and picked him up, cuffing him with flex cuffs on his hands and feet and gagging him. Rafa grabbed the man's wallet and identified him correctly this time, not wanting to have another innocent man on his conscience. This man acted differently than the other too, kind of cocky regardless of the fact that he was obviously disadvantaged, as if they would find out who he worked for and then kiss his ass and let him go. They drove him back to the same abandoned house where they had left the other man. When the target saw the dead man and the way his head was slumped in an awkward position, blood and brains splattered on the wall, the pool of blood on the floor, reality set in. He panicked and tried to hop away from them, but Felix clipped him in the knees with a police baton and the target fell. Felix was laughing.

"Rafa! Wasn't that funny as shit? Guy was like Bugs Bunny!" Rafa smiled, not as amused. His sense of humor was dampened by the sight of the innocent man's body. Sensing his partner's somber mood, Felix shrugged and dragged the target to where the dead man was, and he cut the plastic cuffs that held the cadaver to the chair and pushed the body off. The target shook his head furiously as Felix tried to get him onto the chair, punching him in the stomach several times in the process, and Rafa finally had to help him so that they could strap the guy to the chair. Rafa removed the gag after he was secured, and the man began to scream. Felix laughed crazily, and the man stopped screaming.

"Compadre, there's no one around here. That's why we used this house. No neighbors for at least half a block. And those that are here, well, they know better than to get involved. So you can scream all you like. No one is coming to help."

"I'll tell you anything you want to know!"

Felix grinned and nodded his head. "Oh, I *know* you will."

Felix hadn't been home again for a few days. Julia had been in touch with Rafa and all he said was that they were working. Lila had called and Julia listened to her cry, deep, powerful sobs that brought tears to Julia's eyes as well. Lila couldn't even speak and Julia simply listened on her cell phone and waited for her to calm down.

Julia had not eaten in two days, and she hadn't done any exercise in a week. She slept all day and cried all night. She cried for the happiness she had found with Lila, and for the sadness that had befallen her as well. She often thought she would have been better off not having known Lila, and that way she would not feel the emptiness in her chest that she did now. The only hope she had was this phone call and that she would one day see Lila again. An awful sadness overcame her and she suddenly felt that she may not ever see her lover again.

"Calm down, Lila. What's going on?"

"Felix took my girls! Oh my God, Julia, I don't know what to do."

Julia's heart raced as her mind processed the information that it had just received. She knew Felix could be cruel, but she had no idea that he was capable of this.

"Are you sure?"

"Yes. My babysitter called me. He broke down the door of her house and just took them — at gunpoint! Julia, he's gone mad. What is he going to do with my girls?"

"I haven't seen him in days. I never thought he was capable of this. I'll call him right now."

"No! Don't call him. He'll know we've spoken, and then it could be worse. Please."

"Okay, I won't. You're probably right. I'm so, so sorry Lila."

"This isn't your fault. Felix is crazy. How would you know that?"

"I guess not. I don't know what to do or how to help."

"If you see him, call or text me. If I hear from him, I will let you know. I want to get off the phone now, put it to charge, and hope that he calls me."

"My love, try to stay calm. He probably just wants to scare you."

"He succeeded then. I'm scared to death."

Lila hung up. Julia felt like she weighed a thousand pounds, and she shuffled to her bed and fell onto it. The hole in her chest widened and the emptiness swallowed her up.

16

Lila's cell rang and she answered before it rang a second time. "Hello?"

"Hello, puta."

"Felix, please, let my girls go. I'll do whatever you want."

"Oh, I know you will. Your girls, I wonder if they will take after their mother. I've been thinking what it would be like to tear up some seven-year-old pussy."

Lila gasped. She heard her girls crying in the background. Her heart beat a thousand times a minute. She thought she might faint and tried to get control of herself. "Felix, please!"

"Yeah, they really have some tight little asses, puta. But I'm really not into little girls. Actually, I was thinking that I could make a little cash with these two. Sell them to some rich foreigners. Little virgins go for quite a penny as sex slaves. That would be perfect! Like mother, like daughters."

"Felix-"

"Shut the fuck up and listen!" Felix paused and Lila could almost hear a smile on his face as he spoke again. "I could make some serious cash if I sell them for parts. Kidneys, livers, hearts, shit, I have two healthy girls here- I could make a hundred thousand dollars."

Lila kept quiet, biting her lower lip and holding her fear and tears back. A knot formed in her throat nearly choking her. She tried to swallow but couldn't.

"I'll tell you what. I'm going to think about what I'm going to do for a bit. Then, I'll call you back."

Felix hung up. Lila stared at the phone, motionless, her energy sapped from her, her daughters' lives in a psychopath's hand. She didn't answer the phone when her police captain called, or even when it was Julia. She sat and waited for five hours, and finally, Felix called again.

He didn't wait for her to talk and started in as soon as she picked up the call. "I'm going to do you a huge favor. But I want you to remember how you have felt for the last several hours. I want you to imagine what it would be like not to ever see your daughters again and to always wonder what happened to them. The only reason I don't just kill you is because I doubt Julia would forgive me, and I want her back. But you are going to help me with that, right?"

Julia nodded, then realizing that he couldn't see her, she answered that she would help, however he wanted her to.

"You will end that relationship with her, and now. I'm sure you already have called her and told her what I've done. I really don't care. Call her when we get off the phone and tell her that you have your girls back again. Tell her that you're done with her and that this bullshit is too much for you. Tell her not to do anything that would piss me off. If she does, your girls will pay for it. Tell her to leave things as they are and to forget about you. Convince her, because, and listen good puta. If you don't do what I'm saying, if you ever talk to her or see her again- I promise you, there is no force on this earth that will keep me from your daughters, and I'll make them disappear. Don't think for a minute that the law, the government, or anyone else can help you. You know better, right?"

"Yes." Her mouth was dry and her voice sounded raspy.

"That's right. Now be a good puta, call Julia, and then call me when you're done."

"Okay." She hung up and called Julia. "Julia, I've got my girls back."

"Oh thank God. I didn't think he'd do anything to them. Lila, I can make sure that-"

"No. Listen to me." Lila took a deep breath before continuing. "We're over. I'm not putting up with this kind of shit anymore. I don't need it. Really. You were a good fuck, I enjoyed our time, but it isn't worth it. And don't do anything stupid, because if you do, Felix will hurt my girls, and I could never forgive you for that." Her words left a bitter taste as she said them.

Lila heard Julia sob, then she spoke. "Okay, Lila. I understand. I won't bother you ever again." Julia hung up.

Lila felt awful but called Felix immediately. "It's done."

"Good." He hung up on her.

Lila called back but the call went to voicemail. She called again, and again it went to voicemail. The bastard turned off his phone. Someone knocked on her door, and Lila cursed. "Go away!"

"Mama?"

Lila ran to the door and answered. Her girls were standing in the doorway. Felix was not. She grabbed her girls and slammed and locked the door. She sat hugging them, and all three of them cried together.

17

Felix felt very satisfied as he drove home. Things could finally go back to the way they were. He figured that Julia would be pissed for a bit, but in a few days, or maybe a few weeks, they could go back to being the happy couple that they had been before she had met the puta. He bought some roses from a street vendor at one of the many stop lights on the way. Maybe, he thought, he would even quit seeing other women on the side, turn over a new leaf, so to speak. He arrived at the house, parked the truck, and went in.

The house smelt like burnt tortillas, and Felix went to the kitchen. The corn tortilla that had been left on the comal was burnt black. The fried beans were dry and cracked, also burnt. Julia had left the stove on and was nowhere in sight. Felix shut the stove off and called for her. Julia didn't answer. He thought that maybe she had fallen asleep and he went upstairs to see. The door was slightly ajar and Felix pushed it open. Felix's heart sunk into his stomach as he saw blood dripping from the bed to the floor. Julia was lying down, her hands at her chest and a gun in her right hand. Her face was somber and pale. Felix rushed to her. She had shot herself in the heart with one of the many guns he kept hidden around the home. Felix fell to his knees, the blood staining his pants, and he stared at her. Even in death, she was a beautiful woman. He thought about fucking her one last time, but quickly thought better of it because of how it might look to the forensic team. Felix picked up his cell and called Rafa.

The ambulance, the city cops, the neighbors, and the funeral all were but a blur in the three days that followed Julia's death. Felix had started drinking since he had found Julia dead, and he had not stopped drinking or even slept since. When he was feeling that sleep would overpower his will, he snorted some coke and kept on. He had used coke only a few times in his life, but in just three days he had already gone through two eight balls. He remembered vaguely speaking with friends and relatives but could not recall the exact words exchanged. He felt zombie-like, a shell of the man he was before he drove Julia to her grave. He had tried Lila's number several times, and he called her again. This time a message that the number had been disconnected answered instead. He wanted the puta to know that Julia was dead and that it was her fault. He drove to the Pink Lady and sat in his truck just outside of the bar, parked by the curb, and he cried for the first time since he was three years of age.

He dried his face with a hand towel and got out of the truck, locking it with the remote on the key chain as he entered the Pink Lady. Lila saw him and looked as if she wanted to run, but Felix motioned for her to sit and she obeyed. He sat at the table she was at and ordered a shot of Don Julio tequila. He stayed quiet until the waiter came back, paid the waiter and drank the shot. Lila was trembling.

"Julia's dead."

Lila looked surprised, then her eyes changed and Felix realized that she didn't believe him. He shook his head. "Really, this isn't a trick. She killed herself Sunday. I just wanted you to know that now all the bets are off." Felix got up and left Lila sitting at the table, her mouth open, her cigarette smoldering from its place in the ashtray.

Felix drove to a spot on a hill just outside of Juarez, a place he had taken Julia when they had dated where they would talk, listen to music and make out for hours. He had a bottle of Don Julio and drank from it while he played songs from Los Bukis. He did not feel drunk, just dead inside. The few minutes that he had cried outside of the Pink Lady had left him more emotionally void than ever. He wanted to cry more, feel sadness, anger, something; still, he did not. He simply felt empty. The contents of the bottle of tequila slowly disappeared.

18

"Stop here," Lila told the cab driver when they were but three houses away from Julia's house. She still didn't believe what Felix had told her at the bar and she had to be careful that he didn't find out that she was checking up on Julia. Because her daughters were on vacation visiting their father, she decided to chance it. A woman was sweeping the sidewalk in front of the house where they were parked. "Excuse me," she said to the sweeping woman.

"Yes?"

"Do you know Julia Cañez?"

She stopped sweeping to form the sign of the cross. "I did. That poor girl. And her husband. What a tragedy."

Lila's heart dropped and she swayed a bit. "So, she-died?"

The woman nodded and whispered, "Killed herself."

Lila thanked her, knees buckling, and boarded the cab again.

The driver turned and asked, "Where to?"

"I don't know. Away. Away from here."

The cab driver drove back in the direction where he had picked Lila up, seeming to understand that she was distraught. Her cell rang, and she was going to ignore it, but saw that it was the Captain and answered. She needed a friend, and he was the closest she had to one. Even her coworker Valeria from the Pink Lady was gone; she actually married one of her gringo clients, contrary to Lila's belief that no client would ever take a prostitute seriously.

"Lila, are you crying?"

"Yes. Sorry. Can we meet?"

"Of course we can. How about my place?"

"Okay," she sobbed. She told the driver the address, and after fifteen tear-blurred minutes, they arrived. Lila felt like she was in a nightmare, the driver, the road, the day was all surreal. The Captain was only just arriving himself, and he paid the cab for her before they went into his apartment. Even though he lived alone, his place was always immaculate.

"Sit down," he said motioning to the couch, "I'll fix you a drink."

Lila sat and nodded. She wanted a drink. She wanted several drinks. She watched the Captain serve whiskey and club soda over ice in a medium size glass, and then repeat the operation for himself. He carried the drinks to the couch and sat down with her, handing Lila one as he did. Her hand was shaking and she spilled some of her drink before it got to her mouth.

"Oh God. Sorry."

The Captain shook his head. "Not to worry, Lila. Drink up. It will steady your nerves."

She drank the whiskey in just a few swallows and handed him the glass, and the Captain poured another, stronger than the first. She drank it a little slower. He sat patiently waiting for her to tell him what was wrong without making an issue of it. She finished the second drink and he fixed her a third. Her hands were steadying and she stopped crying.

"Captain, my best friend is dead. She killed herself, and I think it is my fault."

The Captain was pouring whiskey into their glasses. "Someone committing suicide is never someone else's fault. It is a deeply personal decision and depends on no one else's actions. Even if you had done something absolutely terrible to her, which I'm sure isn't the case, your friend made the decision to end her own life, not you."

"I hope you don't judge me, but she was more than a friend."

Without missing a beat, the Captain returned to the couch with the drinks and handed her one. She gladly received it and began to sip. The Captain looked into her eyes and she looked down at her feet. He placed his hand beneath her chin and raised her face gently to meet her eyes again.

"I would never judge you. Lila, I have done terrible things. Much worse than you have ever or could ever do. I am the last person to judge anyone, much less you."

"I loved her. I mean, really, truly loved her. She was married." The Captain listened as Lila related most of the last few weeks' events to him. Afterwards she cried, and he held her. She knew it was wrong to use the Captain this way, but she needed someone, anyone, and he was her best and only option.

19

Felix sat on the bed in his house, running his hand where Julia would have been lying next to him, had she still been alive. He had three weeks of grievance time, but had only asked for a few days. The last thing he wanted was more time to sit and think about her. Over the last few days, he had thought about putting a bullet between his eyes many times over, but he was a coward and was afraid to die. *Now Julia,* he thought, *she had balls, she said fuck it and just did it. There's no way I could do that.* Felix got up from the bed and picked up his pistol from the end table and holstered it. It was time to go back to work. And to hurt someone. The drive to the office felt familiar and comfortable, and it was like everything was back to the way it was, even if only for a moment. Everyone looked at Felix in a strange way when he arrived, and he walked quickly to his desk where Rafa was shuffling through papers. He looked up at Felix, surprised.

"Hey man, what are you doing? You don't need to be here."

"I do. I really do."

Rafa nodded. He put some papers down on the desk and went over to his own desk that was situated in front of Felix's. A manila folder was on the desk and he handed it to Felix. Felix opened it, and a picture of a chubby man in boots and wearing a black Stetson was paper clipped to several papers. Felix looked at Rafa and shrugged. "He's from Sinaloa. Here to take over Chapo's operation downtown."

"This is an official file."

"Yep. And our other boss wants him picked up as well. Dead or alive, we take this guy, and we look good at work and make some extra cash too."

"Sounds like a win/win. Julia could use some new shoes-" Felix stopped in mid-sentence and Rafa looked away.

"Let's go," Felix said.

Rafa nodded. "I think I know where he's at. A place you like, too."

Felix raised his eyebrows, questioning Rafa as to where without saying a word. Rafa smiled. "The massage parlor on Ignacio Mejia. I got a call five minutes before you got in."

"So, who the hell were you going to take with you?"

"I was just wondering exactly that when you came in. I was just looking for your address book to call for some hired help."

"Well, glad I could make it." Felix checked his pistol, ensuring that a round was chambered. "Time is of the essence." Rafa and Felix made their way through the morning traffic, flashing their lights and using the siren in spurts. Their office was only a few minutes away from downtown Juarez. They parked about half a block from the massage parlor. Felix was familiar with the location and knew that there was only one exit in the parlor, which also happened to be the entrance. They loaded up their AR-15s and walked to the parlor. They stood at either side of the door for a moment. Not hearing anything except a soap opera from a television inside, they entered, their assault rifles ready to fire. A woman got up from the couch in the waiting room, sheer terror on her face.

Rafa put a finger to his lips, and she understood to be quiet. She moved quickly out the door. People in Juarez were used to this kind of shit and knew better than to get involved.

The men walked to the adjoining hallway, stopping at each room to listen as they moved down its corridor. In one of the rooms a girl was moaning, a fake sound like the kind that bad porn actresses make. Felix opened the door quietly and peered in. A girl was on top of a portly man, bouncing up and down, her breasts moving with the motion. The man was their target and Felix pointed his weapon at them. The girl saw Felix and screamed, jumping off the massage table, grabbed a towel and ran out of the room, Rafa moving slightly to let her by. The man reached for his pants and Felix sprayed him with bullets. The man's belly shook as the bullets hit him and he fell, dead and bloody.

Rafa laughed. "Hey Felix, if you saw a dude walk in with a weapon pointed at you, would you stop to get a towel around your naked body and then run away, or just run?"

"You mean like that chick?"

"Yeah. I think the last thing I would care about is if someone saw me naked. I mean, shit, she's a whore, what does she care who sees her naked?"

"Beats me. Kind of strange. Call it in, Rafa, will you? I've got a headache."

"Sure."

Felix stared at the dead man's blood on the floor, and his mind's eyes transported him to his house again, Julia bleeding out on their bed and bedroom floor. He shook his head and the vision disappeared, but the awful feeling did not. His stomach ached and his head throbbed, and he stumbled out the door of the parlor and vomited. An old lady walked by and made a face. Felix gave her the finger. She turned and walked away, quickly. Rafa came out and asked if Felix was okay.

"Yeah. I think I might have the flu or something." Rafa stepped back from him.

"You need some time, partner. Losing your wife is heavy shit."

"I'll be alright."

20

Lila watched the Captain sleep while she smoked. He snored, and his round belly moved up and down like a whale submerging and emerging from the ocean. He was sweet to her, but she at best only felt a bit of affection for him. She closed her eyes and pictured Julia's nude body next to her, her muscular legs leading to her round hips, the way her breasts rested on the bed, nipples hard, and her long, black hair flowing over them. She imagined herself turning to look into her deep, emerald eyes and mischievous smile that always melted Lila's heart. Felix's face appeared dark and evil, the son of Satan himself, and Lila flinched, interrupting the Captain's snore.

Lila knew that she was partially at fault, and she also realized that Julia made her decision because she didn't want Felix to do anything to Lila or her daughters, but Felix was definitely the guiltiest of all. She felt hate for someone for the first time in her life. Lila didn't even hate her step father who when she was eight years old had made her do dirty things to him when her mother hadn't been around. She didn't hate the hundreds of men that had entered and exited her life after using her body and acquired talents, calling her derogatory names, and at times being physically abusive to her. Felix, though, she hated. Having threatened her daughters and causing the death of her true love and soul mate, he was more despicable than any of the other men that had ever hurt her before.

The Captain snored loudly and broke her train of thinking. She got out of bed and went to his kitchen to make some coffee. Sleep would not be possible, but she didn't want to go home and be alone, either. So, she sat, smoked and drank coffee until the Captain got up, too, and she acted like a good little wife and made them breakfast. The Captain had a huge smile on his face while he ate his scrambled eggs and tortillas.

"Lila, why don't you and your daughters move in with me." Lila nearly spit out the eggs in her mouth and he smiled. "Really. Think about it. You may not be safe right now. Here you all will be safe and if you want you can look for another place to work. Or just take some time off. I'm doing well right now and I don't mind taking care of you all."

"They'd have to change schools."

"There is a very good private school a block away."

"I can't ask you to do that."

"Honey, you aren't. I'm asking you. It can be a trial basis, no strings attached, and if things don't work out, then I'll even help you move somewhere else. I'm..." he paused and looked down at his now empty plate, "tired of being alone." Lila had just found out that the Captain was a widow. His wife had died of cancer not five years before he started seeing Lila. She found it strange that he had never spoken of it, until he had told her the story the night before. He knew that some guys used their widow status as a way to make girls feel sorry for them and get laid. His Clara would have never accepted that he had explained.

Lila knew that this was an opportunity she might not ever get again. She was getting too old to be a hooker successfully, and she would not likely ever know another love like that of Julia. Her daughters would be upset about moving, but Felix could show up again anytime, and at the very least they'd be in the same city so they could still see their friends now and then. As long as the Captain respected her and her daughters, she couldn't see why the arrangement couldn't work. Even though it was quite contrary to her advice that she had once given to Valeria, her situation called for something drastic. But she would be honest with the Captain so he could never hold it above her head.

"I don't love you. I think very highly of you, even care for you, but I don't love you, and I don't think that it is fair to you."

"I'm aware of that. I also know that you may never love me. And I could be dead tomorrow, next week, and I could have spent some time with a woman that I love and care for, I could have someone to leave my pension to, and could have had a family, the family that I never got to have with Clara. I'm not naïve or stupid. I have always known that you do not love me. But you are sincere and loyal. That's what really matters."

"Okay, Captain, you have a deal. And I have some things I need to give to you. Things that my friend gave me- it's about her husband."

21

Felix had bought a new bed and he slept in the spare bedroom. He had put his house for sale, but it was doubtful that it would sell in Juarez's current market. He had been skipping the gym and only hitting it twice a week for the last few months because it had been one of the things that he and Julia had always tried to do as much as possible as a couple, and people there kept asking about her.

After Felix changed gyms, he started going more regularly. He stopped drinking every day and decided that the only way for him to put Julia's death truly behind him was by killing Lila. She had broken the rules by seeking Julia outside of their paid encounters, and so she was really the one at fault for all of their ensuing problems and Julia's confusion that led to her suicide. He had already looked for Lila and her daughters, and found out that they had moved — a smart move on Lila's part. But if they were still in the city, or in Mexico even, he would find them eventually.

Felix immersed himself in work, the gym, and one-night stands. Killing Lila seemed to be less of a priority with every day that passed. He and Rafa were making a lot of extra cash taking out La Linea's enemies and for the first time in many years, Felix actually had a surplus of money. He decided to buy himself some new boots and headed to a local mall, where one of the best boot shops in Juarez was located. While at the store, he saw Lila and her two girls. All of the murderous feelings that had been subsiding resurfaced.

"Sir?"

Felix turned and stared blankly at the girl that worked at the boot shop.

"I asked you what size you need?"

"Oh. Never mind." He handed the sales girl the boot he was looking at and exited the store, tracking Lila as he did. She hadn't seen him, so he held back a way. She and the girls entered a boutique. He waited outside, because there was only one way in or out. He waited and checked his cell, thirty minutes already. *Why do women take fucking forever shopping, just get what you need and get out already!*

When Lila walked out of the boutique and saw Felix staring at her and the girls, despair befell her soul; she was sure that they were going to die. She reacted, took Carmen and Yamileth by their hands and pulled them right back into the store. Perhaps Felix was crazy enough to kill them in public, in which case it wouldn't matter where they went. Still, she hoped that by being in a public area, they would be safe. Then, she thought of the many times she saw people escape out of bathroom windows in the movies. Or, she could call the Captain, something she really didn't want to do since Felix knew nothing of him, and she knew that information might come in handy later. She dragged her confused daughters to the bathroom in the boutique and shut the door behind them. There were no windows. She started to hyperventilate.

"Mami, what's wrong?" Yamileth looked scared as she asked the question.

"I don't feel well, that's all." Lila concentrated on taking deep, slow breaths and got her breathing and heart rate under control. She walked out of the bathroom, her girls trailing behind her, and out into the boutique. Felix was not there. She walked out to the main mall area and no longer saw Felix. She whirled around crazily, seeing him everywhere and nowhere. She began to doubt that she had seen him at all. Thank God I didn't call the Captain, what would he have thought of me?

She drove the girls to a pizza place close to the Captain's house and bought a pepperoni pizza to go. She watched for anyone that might be following her all the way there, but she saw nothing out of the ordinary.

Felix had really wanted to kill the puta at the mall. He took control of his emotions, and instead, he located her Explorer in the parking lot and waited. She was easy to follow since he was using his motorcycle instead of the unmarked Ram he usually was in. He stayed far behind and nearly lost her, but found the Explorer again when he passed by a pizza joint. He had followed her all the way to a nice house in the San

Lorenzo neighborhood. *How the hell did that puta afford such a nice place?* But now that he knew where she had moved to, he could plan her torture and eventual demise.

He watched her place for a few days and recorded her every move-when she took the girls to school and when she picked them up, when she went to the store. Felix also noted that an older man wearing a city police uniform would leave early every morning and arrive late at night. He wondered if the poor bastard knew that the bitch he had hooked up with was a whore. He took down the plate number and sent a text for Rafa to run it. Felix fantasized about what he'd do. His first order of business would be to sell the puta's girls to the highest bidder. He'd let Lila suffer a few days, and then he would pick her up and take her to a safe house where he would torture her to death. He would wait a few weeks before doing anything and make sure that she didn't see him anywhere; he needed to make sure that Lila was completely off guard when he did it, and that her policeman was nowhere around at the time.

That night, Felix headed to Los Fuentes, a sort of drive-in style bar where narcos and loose women went to meet. He picked up a twenty-year-old hottie, and after a few drinks and lines, they agreed to go somewhere more private. He took her to his house. She had a great body (not as good as Julia's), and he undressed. She took all of him into her mouth, and he was hard as a rock. He hadn't had sex since he had seen Lila at the mall, and he came right away. He pushed her gently onto the bed and licked her body from her neck to her flat belly and continued to her clit. She was wet, and he continued licking and sucking until she came in his mouth. Felix was rock hard again and was about to mount the girl when a sudden flood of memories of Lila and Julia hit him. The girl looked scared.

"Baby, what's wrong?"

He couldn't get the picture of Julia's bucking hips while Lila sucked her pussy out of his head. His cock became flaccid. "Nothing. I just remembered something important I need to do."

The hottie frowned. "I was really hoping for some of this..." she stroked his throbber, "before I left. It was so big!"

Felix let her touch him and she sucked him again, but the images wouldn't go away, and he couldn't get hard again. And now he was getting pissed.

"You know, just go. I've got way too much on my mind now."

"Fine. Your loss."

"Just fucking go!"

The girl got dressed and left. Felix didn't even bother to call a cab for her; he was so annoyed. He never had sexual issues before, and once again, it was Lila's fault. That bitch had to die. He had revised his plan until it was flawless. There was a street along the route she used to take her daughters to school, just a few blocks from her apartment, which had a major dip at a cross section. She had no choice but to slow down at that spot and he would be parked on the crossroad and would hit her as she crossed. He would use an old Ford, the heavy all steel kind from the seventies, that he had borrowed from the impound lot. He also had a burn phone that he would give to Lila so he could make calls to her after he had the girls. No matter what he would sell the girls, but he would make her think that she still had a chance to save them and would use that to lure her to wherever he wanted her to go. Once she was under his power, he would make sure that she knew the fate of her daughters and would torture her both physically and mentally as long as he felt like it. *Tomorrow*, he thought, *tomorrow is the day*. Felix masturbated while imagining raping and torturing Lila. He finally came.

22

"Hurry up, Yamileth! Carmen is already eating, and we are going to be late because of you, young lady!"

Lila had served her girls scrambled corn tortilla and eggs. The Captain had left very early, muttering about some special operation he was in charge of. He had been very quiet the last few weeks after she told him that she thought she had seen Felix. He kept going over the information that she had given to him about Felix. He was obviously upset that she hadn't called him right away when she had possibly seen him. The girls finally finished eating, and after brushing their teeth she inspected them both. They looked lovely in their school uniforms, and they climbed into the Explorer and left for school. Carmen was running her mouth as usual as Lila slowed down for a dip in the road and her cell rang.

Felix had been sitting at his strategic spot on the crossroad since six in the morning. He wanted to make sure that he didn't miss her even if she left earlier than she normally did, around seven-fifteen. It was getting closer to seven, and he was getting impatient, but he imagined the look on Lila's face as he tore her children from her wrecked SUV and threw her the cell, and he felt calmer. He would have so much fun with that bitch while he made her believe that she might actually get to save her whore daughters. He had a huge smile on his face and didn't even notice that a black Expedition had pulled up behind and slightly to the side of his borrowed pickup.

Felix turned and saw five men surrounding the truck, all with AK-47s. The cop he had seen at Lila's house was ordering other men to surround the truck. *Fuck*, he thought, *now I won't be able to kill the puta*! Felix pulled out his .45 and started firing at the cop man and his crew. They opened fire on Felix, their AKs shredding him and the truck he was in. He felt the bullets rip through his face, neck and chest, and felt his blood pour out of him, and a bullet hit his brain and he felt no more. A text message buzzed Felix's cell.

The Captain grabbed Felix's hand, pulled out a hunting knife, chopped off a finger and stuck it in a Ziploc bag. He returned the knife to its sheath and pocketed the finger. He heard the cell phone in Felix's pocket buzz and he fished it out of his pocket. He read the message that had just been received.

Caution! That dude is a police captain that works for El Chapo- he's known as

The Butcher because he likes to take body parts as trophies…

The Captain laughed. He pocketed the phone and pulled out his own phone to call Lila.

23

"Captain?" Lila was surprised to hear from him this early.

"Lila, my love, look to your right as you drive past the corner."

She did. An old bullet-ridden pickup was at the corner, and she noticed the figure of a man slumped in the driver's seat, and blood, lots of blood. The Captain was standing nearby, out of uniform, and waived at her as she passed.

"That's Felix Cañez. Lucky for us he works for La Linea, and I, well, don't, so my boss put a hit on him as soon as I gave him the information you had given me. I've had my men following him for the last few weeks. I'm pretty sure he was going to try to kill you today, and that's why he was at this location. I would have said something, darling, but I needed you to be calm and not change your route. I hope you aren't mad, but I promise you that I never let you and the girls out of my sight. At least it's over, Lila."

She wasn't mad at all. "Thank you." Lila smiled and thought of Julia, and, for the first time since Felix had taken her daughters, she felt peace. After she dropped off the girls, Lila went to the cemetery where she had learned that Julia was buried. It took her a few hours, but when she found Julia's gravestone, she sat down with two cups of coffee and tamales.